"I wonder what yo... *passion against hu*... ... *a different direction," A*... *used aloud, his shocking blue eyes pinning her to the spot.*

Maggie reeled under the impact of his stare, felt herself drowning in his gaze, a willing victim going down for the third time and loving every minute of it. Then, with superhuman effort she mentally pulled herself free of the hypnotic effect he had on her. "You'll never know, you . . . you barbarian!"

He reached for her with the swiftness of a night hawk, and his hard lips took possession of hers. His strong arms pulled her against his body, and even through all their layers of clothing she could feel his muscled strength.

Warmed by his kiss, her chilled lips opened and moved, slowly, sensuously at first, and then in a fever of undisguised passion. Maggie knew she was courting danger. But she clung to Adam a while longer, skirting the edge of the chasm, unwilling to plunge over the edge—and unable to pull away. . . .

WHAT ARE *LOVESWEPT* ROMANCES?

They are stories of true romance and touching emotion. We believe those two very important ingredients are constants in our highly sensual and very believable stories in the *LOVESWEPT* line. Our goal is to give you, the reader, stories of consistently high quality that may sometimes make you laugh, sometimes make you cry, but are always fresh and creative and contain many delightful surprises within their pages.

Most romance fans read an enormous number of books. Those they truly love, they keep. Others may be traded with friends and soon forgotten. We hope that each *LOVESWEPT* romance will be a treasure—a "keeper." We will always try to publish

*LOVE STORIES YOU'LL NEVER FORGET
BY AUTHORS YOU'LL ALWAYS REMEMBER*

The Editors

One

The four-wheel-drive pickup truck skidded on a patch of ice as it barreled along Highway 30 toward the Tallahatchie River. Maggie fought with the wheel, swearing under her breath, brought the truck back under control, and glanced at her watch. If she didn't hurry she'd be too late. It was already five A.M., and thirty minutes before sunrise the hunters would emerge from their blinds, blasting ducks from the sky, ducks just like Donald and Baby Huey, her two pets.

She stepped on the gas and prayed as the truck careened off the highway and onto a winding dirt road. The bumpy road jarred her teeth as she bounced through the Holly Springs National Forest on her way to the river. In the predawn gloom, the trees looked like giant, silent ghosts. Maggie ignored the primeval beauty of the forest as she squinted for her first glimpse of the river. There it was, just ahead, its waters dim and murky in the darkened forest.

Maggie squealed to a halt and jumped out. The twenty-degree weather blasted her, turning her nose a bright pink.

"Damn," she muttered. "Forgot my hat." She immediately scrambled back inside the warm cab of her truck and felt along the seat for her wool toboggan cap. Pulling it down over her wild tangle of honey-colored hair, she stepped back out into the wintry chill.

Maggie sprinted to the rear of her truck and lowered the tailgate. Using all the strength her athletically toned body could muster, coupled with sheer, stubborn determination, she dragged the aluminum rowboat onto the ground and toward the river. She shoved it into the water, where it landed with a plop like an ungainly, silver-bellied fish. She started to climb in and stopped. "Damn. Forgot my trumpet." She pulled the boat back up on the bank and hurried over to her truck.

The silver trumpet, pride of her high-school marching-band days, lay in its case. With tender pride she took it from the case and rubbed its shiny sides. "Baby, we're going to make beautiful music today."

A wicked grin played about Maggie's full, sensuous lips as she pushed the boat back into the water and stepped in, setting her trumpet beside her. Taking the oars in her hands, she rowed toward the center of the river. The dark waters lapped against the sides of the boat as it moved swiftly under Maggie's expert stroking.

She rounded a bend in the river and headed toward a wide, open space that would give her a clear view of the ducks as they came in for a landing.

She put the oars in the bottom of the boat and sat shivering, waiting for the first sound that would herald the start of the battle. Out of the gloom it came, a hoarse cry from the west bank of the river, the low, urgent sounds of a hunter's duck call.

She reached for her trumpet, her muscles tensed in anticipation. Her fingers, sticking out of the holes Maggie had cut in the ends of her gloves, clutched the icy trumpet. She dreaded putting the cold metal to her lips, but she would do anything for her cause.

Maggie held her breath, straining to hear the approach of the ducks. From high in the sky came the first answering calls as the ducks approached the river in a V formation, winging their way toward destruction.

Putting the trumpet to her lips, Maggie sounded the opening bars of the *William Tell* overture. The brazen notes echoed through the silent forest, rising clear and loud in the morning air. The ducks that had begun their descent toward the river rose in alarm and soared back up into the sky.

From the west bank the blast of a shotgun sounded. Maggie watched in glee as the shot missed its mark. Not a single feather floated downward.

Maggie stood up, planted her feet firmly apart in the swaying boat, and yelled, "Hi-ho, Silver! Away!" Her lips were already numb from contact with the icy trumpet, but she didn't care. The victory was hers. Triumphantly, she once more played the opening bars of what had become the Lone Ranger's theme. Without the urgency of the first time, the music took on a clarity and precision that had been her hallmark in high school and college. It was a skill that had enabled her not only to play a "boy's" instrument, but to outshine all the boys who'd played it.

"What the hell's going on out there!" The enraged voice rose from a duck blind on the west bank of the river, and was followed by the appearance of a hunter of gigantic proportions, dressed from head to toe in camouflage green. His twenty-gauge shotgun was unbreached and slung across his shoulder.

"I've saved the ducks from assassination," she yelled. She still stood tall in her aluminum boat, and if she had been on dry land she would have swaggered. The freezing trumpet dangled from her hand.

"Are you crazy? Get off this river before you get shot."

"The assassin has scruples, does he?" Maggie taunted.

"Damned activist!" he roared back.

"You bet your smoking twenty-gauge I'm an activist!" Maggie rubbed her coat sleeve across her red nose to restore some circulation. The boat rocked from her slight movement, but she steadied it by shifting the position of her nearly frozen feet.

"This is duck season. Get off that river!" The hunter had moved to the edge of the water, closer to her drifting boat, close enough that she could see his face. It was vaguely familiar. Something about that strong, square jaw triggered a faint memory, but she couldn't quite capture it.

"Try telling that to the ducks. They don't know there's a murder plot and they are the intended victims."

While they were arguing, dawn had crept over the forest. The branches of the trees were tipped with pink and gold as the faint December sun spread its feeble warmth across the wooded hills of northeast Mississippi. The waters of the Tallahatchie River changed from murky gray to deep blue.

"Victims, hell! Now, get off that river before you freeze your butt."

"Not until you put away that shotgun." The boat had drifted closer to the bank, and she could see that the hunter's eyes were deep blue, as blue as the Tiffany favrile glass goblet sitting on the windowsill in her kitchen catching the sun. Beneath his camouflage safari hat, his black eyebrows were drawn together in a fierce scowl. She chuckled with malicious glee. Good, she thought. He was so mad at her that he had completely forgotten about slaughtering ducks. She clapped her nearly frozen hands together to get the circulation going.

"You must be insane. I'm here to hunt."

"And I'm here to see that you don't."

"Just who the hell do you think you are?"

"I don't think, I know. I'm Maggie Merriweather, president and founder of Friends of the Animals, at your service." She lifted her trumpet to her lips and blasted forth a high C. She chuckled as the hunter stepped back and muttered a word that would curl the ears of her second-grade students at East Heights Elementary.

A lone green-head mallard that had drifted in, unnoticed, stretched his iridescent neck in fright and lifted over the Tallahatchie River. The hunter reached for his gun, but he was too late. By the time he had loaded, breached, and aimed his gun, the male duck was out of range. The hunter shot into the air just on principle.

The bow of Maggie's boat was now touching the west bank of the river. She could see the outrage plainly stamped on the hunter's handsome face. A line of anger was etched around his lips. A name stirred in the back of her memory, a name associated with a newspaper story from about a year ago. If it weren't for that hat, she might have been able to identify her adversary.

Maggie sat down in her boat and guided it in, consumed now with curiosity to learn the identity of the good-looking madman standing on the bank. She forgot the bitter cold in her quest for his identity.

He stood with folded arms and watched her drag the aluminum boat onto the shore. With lithe sureness, Maggie secured the boat, grabbed her trumpet from the boat seat, and turned to face her foe.

"Well, Ms. Merriweather—and I'm sure a woman of your persuasions insists on being addressed as Ms.—you've succeeded in ruining a good morning's hunt for me."

"Well, now, Mr.—" Maggie stopped, hoping he would supply his name. He stood like a rock before her, his lips clamped shut in a tight line. Before the pause became too obvious, she continued speaking. "I've saved more than a few of my feathered friends from being mounted and hung on some wall for display."

"What you've done today is deprive me of my supper."

"How touching," she said sarcastically.

"Yes, Ms. Merriweather, you've saved that duck from the stew pot." His blue eyes glared at her.

"Why don't you try carrots?" she suggested.

"Do I look like a rabbit to you?"

"No, but I'll bet you'd like to put a cute little Easter bunny in that stewpot of yours too."

"Bravo, Ms. Merriweather. How discerning of you."

"Damned barbarian!" she replied hotly.

"Addlepated activist!"

"Well, at least I don't hide my identity," she shouted. Who was he, she wondered, this superbly built man towering over her? Why, he had to be at least six feet four to stand so tall above her own five nine. She had to find out who he was. She liked to know the names of her enemies.

"I didn't hear you ask my name. But then, your manners do leave a lot to be desired." He casually lifted his gun.

"What are you going to do, shoot me?"

A devil-may-care, pirate's grin split his handsome, sun-bronzed face. "That's not a bad idea," he said as he unbreached his gun once more. "Actually, I had figured on telling you my name, since you're so all-fired determined to know it."

He pushed his hat back on his head, and Maggie noticed his hands. They were well-kept, the fingernails nicely manicured. They were the hands of a man who worked indoors. Like a banker . . . that was it! He was—

"Adam Trent," he drawled. "And I'll probably live to rue the day I told when you come marching onto my front lawn with protest signs."

He was the youngest man ever to become president of Mutual Bank, Maggie recalled. That was why his face was familiar. Nearly a year ago the local paper had done a story about his phenomenal rise to success. He looked better in person than he did in print, she decided.

"Marching on lawns is not my style." Maggie brandished her silver trumpet at him. "I go for the jugular vein."

"As you can see, Ms. Merriweather, I'm not bleeding."

"I wouldn't speak too soon, Mr. Trent. This is only opening day. My cohorts and I intend to make these woods hell for hunters."

"Well, just keep out of my way, Ms. Merriweather. I'm not a patient man, and I don't like damned activists." He turned his back on her and muttered, "No matter how good-looking they are."

"And I don't like hunters. If you plant your hunting boots in these woods, Mr. Trent, be prepared to do battle with me." She flung the words at his broad, stiff back as she stamped her aching feet on the ground trying to warm them. She was willing to give up plenty for her cause, but she didn't plan on giving up her feet.

He whirled back around at her words. "Are you challenging me, Ms. Merriweather?"

"Precisely, Mr. Trent."

"Then prepare to get a dent in your horn." With that parting shot he grabbed his empty game bag and disappeared into the woods.

Never one to let somebody else have the last word, Maggie lifted the trumpet to her blue lips and played "Taps." "That's for you and every hunter like you," she yelled into the silent forest. Her only answer was the revving of a cold engine in the distance.

With adrenaline pumping like fire in her veins from the thrill of the first victory of the hunting season, Maggie dragged her boat back to her truck and began the arduous task of maneuvering it aboard. She put all one hundred twenty pounds of herself to bear on the task, and, with a fierce will, managed to get it accomplished. With the boat secure, Maggie climbed into the cab of her four-wheel-drive and headed home to Belden.

She was whistling and humming, clipping down Highway 30 doing seventy, when she heard the siren behind her. "Well, shoot," she muttered as she pulled off the road. "Who would have thought they'd be out this early in the morning?"

"Going to a fire, lady?" The blue-coated officer of the Mississippi Highway Patrol grinned at her.

"You caught me red-handed, sir. Just please don't cart me off to jail." Maggie smiled her most engaging smile, the one that changed her face from merely pretty to stunning. Sometimes flirting helped, and she wasn't above trying.

"Your driver's license, please, ma'am." He looked unimpressed.

Maggie groaned. She thought of the chunk this ticket would take out of her paltry schoolteacher's pay.

After the dastardly deed was done, Maggie

started her truck on its way: formerly a blue streak of lightning, it now resembled a blue snail. She inched her way back to her country cottage on the lake and parked in her garage. Sam and Muffin and Frisky barked joyous greetings to her and followed her inside for their usual tidbits.

Frisky Beagle's toenails clicked on the brick floor as he did his whirling-dervish dance. Maggie chuckled and reached into the cabinet for the dog biscuits. Her eyes fell on the Tiffany favrile glass goblet on her windowsill, which was catching the morning sun. Her hands stopped in midair as she watched the sun sparkle on the deep sapphire glass and cast a brilliant blue reflection across her white curtains. Fascinated, she decided Adam Trent's eyes were exactly the color of that goblet. She dreamily put the copper kettle on to boil.

There is only so much waiting a dog will stand. Frisky's sharp bark brought Maggie back to the matter at hand. Good land! she thought. Whatever had possessed her to be standing there like a moron, thinking of Adam Trent's eyes? She rummaged around in the half-empty box and came up with biscuits for Frisky, Sam, and Muffin. Wagging their tails greedily, they disappeared out the doggie door, a hinged affair in the bottom of Maggie's kitchen door. She laughed as Muffin struggled to squeeze her chubby behind through the small door.

Leaning over, Maggie lifted the hinged door and called to the obese bulldog, "I'm going to have to put you on a diet, Muffin."

Muffin lifted her pug nose in disdain and marched to the other side of the garage, totally ignoring that outrageous suggestion.

Maggie peeled off her cap and parka and her heavy boots. Then she began to work on her second layer of clothes. She was down to a pair of baggy army pants and a red sweat shirt when Martha Jo came breezing through her patio door.

Plopping herself into a kitchen chair and propping her tiny feet on the table, she looked Maggie up and down and gave a small nod of satisfaction. "Tell me all about the victory," she commanded. The wind had turned Martha Jo's red hair upside-down and given it the appearance of a rag mop on top of her head.

"Don't you ever say 'hi'?" Maggie scolded her as she put the tea up to steep.

"Hi, and tell me everything that happened, and what does a poor little ole girl like me have to do to get a cup of coffee?" Martha Jo plunked her feet down on the floor with a loud bang and propped her elbows on the table.

"You know I don't drink coffee. If you want coffee, go to the truck stop."

"What! And expose this body to the view of all those lecherous old men?" She wiggled her bottom in her size-fourteen slacks and laughed.

Maggie poured two cups of steaming orange spice tea and joined her friend and fellow schoolteacher at the sun-washed antique table. "I got up at four o'clock this morning, loaded my trusty trumpet into the pickup, and drove forty miles in the dark to Tallahatchie River bottom."

"Your devotion to the cause touches my heart." Martha Jo took a sip of her tea. "This stuff is awful. When are you going to start serving a decent cup of coffee?"

"Beggars can't be choosers."

"Aw, come on, Maggie." Martha Jo took another sip of tea and made a wry face. "If I live to be a hundred I might get used to it. Then what happened?"

"It was perfect." Maggie's green cat's eyes sparkled in the early morning sunlight as she talked. "The ducks came in and I scared them clear to

Mexico with my trumpet." She and Martha Jo laughed heartily at the success of the mission.

"Were there any hunters there?"

"Just one." Maggie bent over her cup and looked smug, knowing that Martha Jo was dying to know more.

The grandfather clock ticked loudly in the corner of the kitchen as the minutes stretched out. Maggie sipped her tea and waited.

Finally Martha Jo could stand the suspense no longer.

"Well, for Pete's sake! Who was it?" she exploded.

"Adam Trent."

"Adam Trent? Tupelo's wonder-boy banker? Mississippi's most eligible bachelor?" She groaned and raked her fingers through her mop of hair. "Why didn't I go with you?"

Maggie laughed. "You said you wouldn't get out of bed at four o'clock on Saturday morning for anybody except the President of the United States."

"Isn't that just my luck? While I'm innocently sleeping my life away, you're in the woods with a heartthrob!"

"Does that mean you're going with the pot-and-pan brigade next Saturday?" Maggie was referring to the group of Friends of the Animals who planned to march through the woods in Boguefala Bottom, beating on pots and pans, to foil the first deer hunt of the season.

"Wild horses couldn't keep me away."

"Then, drink your tea. You'll need your strength," Maggie told her.

Martha Jo rose and yanked her hat down over her ears. "Ugh. Keep your brew. I'm going home for a cup of good coffee. See you at school tomorrow." She banged breezily out the kitchen door and disappeared in the direction of her cottage, next door.

Maggie stretched and yawned. "If I don't get my circulation going, I'll fall asleep." She walked over to the coatrack to get her parka, and her eyes fell on the blue goblet. Adam's eyes. Her hand absently caressed one puffy sleeve as the goblet winked at her in the sun. She grabbed her coat and whirled out the door as if pursued by demons.

Whistling for her dogs, she ran toward the lake behind her house. The wind lifted her honey-colored mane of hair and swept it back from her ears. She clamped her hands over her ears and shivered.

"Damn. Forgot my hat."

Two

On Tuesday Maggie called Mac Jennings. It was surprisingly painless.

"I need to borrow the nursing-home van tomorrow after school."

"You must be crazy," he told her.

"That's what you said last spring when you jilted me." She grinned into the telephone. After she'd gotten through hating Mac last May, she'd fallen out of love with him, and now they were just good friends.

"Well, what did you have in mind?" the suspicious director of the Deerfield Nursing Home asked.

"I'm going to take my Wednesday-afternoon bingo ladies on an outing."

"Maggie, is this for one of your causes?"

The telephone scorched her hand when Mac said "causes." He'd hated her causes. When he'd broken their engagement he'd cited her causes as the main reason. "I just can't cope with it anymore,

Maggie," he had said. "I want a wife, not a modern-day Joan of Arc who stomps all over northeast Mississippi toting signs and tooting horns." He didn't like dogs, either. It was a good thing they'd broken up, Maggie had to admit.

"Just have my bingo ladies ready to travel tomorrow at three-thirty, Mac. They'll love it."

"Maag-gie," he said, a warning in his voice.

"Now, Mac," she cajoled him, "how many years have I been coming to Deerfield on Wednesday afternoons to play bingo? Since I was twenty-five. Right, Mac? Three whole years. Now, Mac, in all that time have I ever brought any harm to those dear, sweet ladies?"

"There was the time on the Natchez Trace Parkway when that forest ranger caught you and those sweet little ladies red-handed, stealing bodock apples."

"Not stealing. Just borrowing to use for crafts."

"On government property, Maggie."

"Well, he let us go when I explained how those dear, sweet nursing-home residents wanted to make Halloween witches with the bodock apples. He even let us keep the apples."

Mac heaved a resigned sigh. Maggie knew she had won.

On Wednesday afternoon, she loaded thirteen lively little gray-haired ladies into the Deerfield Nursing Home van and headed for Holly Springs National Forest.

Mac stood on the front lawn in the near-freezing weather and practically wrung his hands as she drove off.

"Maggie, what's this gun doing back here?" piped up Mrs. Peabody as she bounced around on the back seat.

"I'll explain later, Mrs. Peabody. Gotta get gas."

She took a sharp right turn off West Main Street and squealed into Tupelo Savings Station, narrowly missing a parked silver Mercedes. The license plate on the back of the luxury car read "ADAM 1."

Maggie hitched up her baggy army pants, pulled her toboggan cap low over her green eyes, and jumped down from the driver's seat.

Adam Trent bailed out of his car, all spit and polish in a gray pin-striped suit. "I might have known it would be you." He looked grim. "Do you always drive like a maniac?"

Maggie caught her breath at the sight of him. Gracious, she thought, just look at those shoulders in that perfectly tailored suit. It had to be a sin to hide a body like that under clothes.

"Are you always so serious? Loosen up, Adam, or you'll get ulcers." She jerked the hose from the gas pump marked "Premium, Unleaded" and never even noticed that she had called him "Adam."

Adam leaned casually against the side of the van and watched as she filled the tank with gas. "Tell me . . . Maggie, isn't it? . . . what makes you tick?"

"A heart. Just like everybody else." A marshmallow heart. That was what her brother called it. As a young girl she used to cry over every broken, suffering animal brought into her father's veterinary clinic. She believed that animals should be healthy and alive, running free in the sun, flying high in the wind. It was inconceivable to her that anyone could be heartless enough to use a gun to snuff out the life of a living creature.

"Oh, come now, Maggie," Adam chided her, relaxing against the van as if he owned it and everybody connected with it. "There's more to you than meets the eye." His Tiffany-glass blue eyes boldly raked her from head to toe, taking in the lopsided knit cap, the down parka that zipped with room to spare over her slim torso, the baggy army pants that almost disguised her long, shapely legs.

Maggie was mesmerized by his eyes. While her

hands were pumping gasoline into the tank, her mind was spiraling off on a breathless tangent. Did he have hair on that magnificent chest, hidden away behind that flawless white shirt? Did he have three mistresses tucked away in his bed to keep all his shirts so white? He was so close she could see a small muscle twitching in the side of his perfectly formed square jaw. A man like him had to have a mistress or two panting in the vaults of that staid old bank of his, Maggie was certain. It wasn't fair, not fair at all that he should look like a Greek god and have sixteen gorgeous mistresses whom she hated, and live worlds away from her. Nobody—before, including, and after Mac—had excited her imagination the way Adam Trent did.

"What makes a woman like you go into the woods before dawn to fight for the animals?" She noticed when he spoke that even his teeth were perfect.

"What makes you stand here in thirty-degree weather and ask? Don't you have a bank, or something, to run?" She would have to tread cautiously around him, Maggie reminded herself. He was, after all, the enemy. But then, why was she just itching to pull the shirt off her enemy to see if he had hair on his chest?

"I'm curious. More than curious, actually. After all, you did cheat me out of a duck supper Saturday." When he smiled, Maggie was sure that every Christmas candle in Tupelo had dissolved right down to its wick. "What kind of woman are you? What are you hiding under all those baggy clothes?"

Maggie had a coughing fit. Good land! she thought wildly. She was standing there wanting to undress him and he was standing there wanting to see under her clothes! And he didn't even have the good grace to turn red in the face as he made his outrageous remark.

Thirteen noses pressed against the windows of

the van, and thirteen pairs of lively eyes watched in fascination as gasoline overflowed the tank and spilled unnoticed over Maggie's hands. Thirteen gray heads nodded approvingly as the handsome man took the overflowing hose from the beautiful woman and hung it back on the gas pump. Thirteen wrinkled faces smiled in delight as the hero took a chamois rag off the rack beside the pumps and rubbed the gasoline from the heroine's hands. The residents of Deerfield Nursing Home loved romance.

Maggie's marshmallow heart melted right down to her toes when Adam took her hands in his. As those fine, strong hands dabbed at the gasoline she pictured herself on a beach in Tahiti with those hands rubbing coconut oil over her bronzed body. "I can do that for myself," she protested, but not too strongly.

His smile lit up the entire west side of Tupelo. "We can't let anything happen to your hands, can we, now, Maggie? Then you wouldn't be able to toot your horn."

"I should think you'd be happy if I never played my trumpet again. All things considered." They were now lying together on the white, hot sands, their well-oiled limbs entangled. She peered up at his face from under her wool cap. She wondered if he read minds. Lord, she hoped not!

"I should have told you Saturday. I love a good fight with a worthy adversary."

"Even when you're bested?"

"Even then."

The job of cleaning her hands had become quite an undertaking. Not that Maggie was complaining. While Adam studiously concentrated on each long, tapered finger, she was blushing at what the two of them were now doing on that beach in Tahiti.

He began rubbing her gasoline-free, ice-cold

hands between his. "Don't expect to win every time, Maggie."

"Oh, but I do." The steamy heat rose from that fantasy beach and smote her in the midriff, radiating in waves throughout her body. She felt so overheated she considered shucking her coat right there in the gas station, in the middle of December. Just peeling it off and fanning herself right there in front of everybody.

"And are these the cohorts who will be helping you?" Adam's hand waved to encompass the van full of fascinated gray-haired ladies.

Maggie dragged herself off the beach, scorched and seared, and pulled her fractured mind together. Adam must not suspect the nature of this afternoon's outing, she reminded herself. Laughing shakily, she told him, "These are my Wednesday-afternoon bingo partners from Deerfield Nursing Home."

"You play bingo in the van?"

"Of course not. Sometimes we don't play bingo."

"What do you do when you don't play bingo?"

"We go on little outings."

"In thirty-degree weather? Isn't it a mite cold for them to be on an outing?"

"They like excitement."

Adam's deep, rich laugh filled the winter air. "Then, tell them for me that they've come to the right person. I don't know anybody better able to generate excitement than you."

"Thank you."

"I'm not sure I meant it as a compliment." His smile raised the temperature outside the gas station at least fifteen degrees. "I hope they're all heavily insured. Riding in boats on the Tallahatchie River can be dangerous." With those words, he turned to go inside the station. When he had gone a few feet from her, he swiveled halfway around and spoke over his shoulder. "Maggie, try not to run over my car when you leave. I'm kind of partial to it."

"I was considering leaving just a small dent." She grinned impishly at him.

"That's probably the truth." He walked away, and there was a great big empty place where he had been standing.

Maggie shivered. Suddenly she realized how cold she was. She hopped back inside the warm van and stuck her numbed hands next to the heater.

"Who is he, Maggie?" Mrs. Peabody called from the back.

"My, my, he's handsome," Mrs. Vinson said.

"He made this old girl swoon," added Mrs. Clark.

"Fannie Mae, I didn't know you had it in you," Mrs. Vinson said to Mrs. Clark.

Mrs. Clark laughed. "Emma, just because there's snow on the roof doesn't mean there's no fire in the oven."

Maggie turned to face them. "That, ladies, is the enemy. Adam Trent. He's one of the hunters I've sworn to foil." She paused to let the truth sink in. At last Wednesday's bingo game she had presented her cause to the ladies of Deerfield, and they had all begged to be part of the plan. Such excitement rarely came their way.

After the chorus of "Oh, my's" and "Dear me's" had subsided, Maggie went on. "Today we're going hunting." There was a collective gasp, and then she added, "Today will go down in history as one of the most unsuccessful hunts ever attempted. I doubt that a single duck or bird or squirrel or rabbit or deer will be killed." There were chuckles of appreciation from her co-conspirators. "What we are going to do today is stuff the application box, so that when the one-day antlerless deer season is declared and names are drawn for the limited number of permits, guess whose names will be drawn."

"Absolutely ingenious, Maggie," Mrs. Vinson cried.

"I haven't had this much fun since we stole the bodock apples," added Mrs. Clark.

Maggie sat down behind the wheel, revved the engine, and took her excited crew to the Holly Springs National Forest. She pulled up at one of the entrances to the hunting area, got fourteen hunting forms, and brought them back to the van.

"If anyone needs a pencil, just yell."

"Maggie, what do we put on this line that asks what we're hunting?" Mrs. Peabody asked.

"Well, I should think that any of the game animals would do." She worked quickly, filling out her form, and then stood up in the front of the van. "On the line that asks for number bagged, put zero. We don't want to confuse anybody about the number of animals killed, we just want the lion's share of permits so that as few as possible will be killed."

After they had filled out the forms at that entrance, Maggie raced around to a second entrance and repeated the process. "Ladies, if anybody ever asks you what kind of gun you used, it's right back there. It's a twenty-gauge. It's too bad all of you are such poor shots."

The merriment in the van was running high by the time they had filled out forms at four different entrances to the hunting areas. The sun had disappeared over the edge of the forest when Maggie turned the van toward Tupelo.

"Can we do this next Wednesday?" Mrs. Clark asked.

"It's a lot more fun than bingo," Mrs. Peabody added.

"If I can beg or borrow the van from Mac, we'll do it again next Wednesday," Maggie promised.

"You could steal the van. Temporarily, of course," Mrs. Vinson suggested.

"Emma, I'm shocked at you," Mrs. Clark said with a gasp.

"Well, it's no worse than you, Fannie Mae. Fires in the oven, indeed. Why, Mr. Trent wouldn't look once at old fossils like you and me," Mrs. Vinson said with a sniff.

"Who said anything about Mr. Trent?" Mrs. Clark looked smug.

"Have you been carrying on with Mr. Luther, down the hall?"

Fannie Mae Clark burst into laughter. "No. I'm just trying to get a rumor started. You know, spice things up a little."

Maggie headed into the Deerfield Nursing Home parking lot and deposited her chattering crew at the door. She handed the van's keys over to Mac.

"I see the van and my residents are still in one piece," he remarked.

"What did you expect?" Maggie asked him, grinning.

"I don't know, Maggie. With you, anything is possible."

"Cheer up, Mac. Maybe Santa Claus will stuff your stocking with a nice, boring girl." She turned to leave and then remembered. "Oh, Mac. I'll want the van again next Wednesday."

"I'm not even going to ask why."

Maggie reached over and pinched the pained expression on his face. "See you Wednesday, Mac." She stuffed her hands into her pants pockets and jogged out to her pickup truck. The cold engine caught after a couple of tries, and Maggie took the bypass home to Belden.

A stack of ungraded second-grade papers greeted Maggie when she walked in the door of her cozy cottage. She tossed her coat in the general direction of the coatrack, missed, stooped over to pick it up, and caught a lingering whiff of gasoline. She stood in the middle of her kitchen floor with the faint odor of gasoline on her hands and remembered Adam. The way he laughed, the way he walked, the way he stood next to her, the way his hands felt on hers.

In slow motion, she hung the jacket up and floated toward the kitchen sink. She had to reach the soap dish. That gasoline on her hands had obviously affected her brain. She scrubbed her hands until they were bright pink and smarting. Leaning over, she sniffed them. There was not the slightest trace of gasoline. Good. That meant she had washed Adam down the sink drain.

Three

Maggie led the way in her pickup truck as the Friends of the Animals descended on Boguefala Bottom. The temperature had dropped another five degrees, making the December weather unusually cold for Mississippi. To add to the discomfort, a slow, drizzling rain had started to fall.

Martha Jo Peterson, sitting beside Maggie in the truck, yawned hugely. "I'm going to be furious if I've gotten up at the crack of four and Adam Trent doesn't show up."

"Are you here to save the animals or to ogle Adam?" Maggie would have to be tarred and feathered before she would admit that she had spent the last two days wondering whether Adam would be among the deer hunters in Boguefala Bottom for the opening day of the season. She alternated between hoping he would be there and praying he would not. For all she knew he could be hunting down in Clay County or over in Itawamba. The Friends had chosen Boguefala simply because in past years it had recorded more deer bagged on opening day than any other area in northeast Mississippi.

"I'm planning to do both," Martha Jo told her. "While I'm stomping through the woods beating my pizza pan, I'm also going to be beating the bushes for Trent."

"Don't get your hopes up. He doesn't like activists."

Martha Jo laughed. "He doesn't have to like activists. I'm not planning to marry the guy, just ogle him some and maybe pant and paw over him a little."

"I call that consorting with the enemy."

"Party-pooper."

Maggie parked the truck by the side of Boguefala Creek. She and Martha Jo waited inside the warm truck for the rest of the pot-and-pan brigade to arrive. When everybody had finally assembled, Maggie took her metal soup spoon and her stainless-steel pot and hopped down from the truck.

"You all know what to do," she told the crowd. "We'll spread out and march through the woods, making as much noise as we can. By the time we've made our sweep, there won't be any deer within fifteen miles of this place." She reached into the back of her truck and pulled out a hot-pink vest. "If anybody needs a vest, I have plenty in the back of my truck. I don't want anybody getting shot."

"How long should we stay, Maggie?" Carl Lamons asked.

"I grew up around here, and I'm sure we can cover this section of woods in less than an hour. It's too cold to stay much longer than that anyhow."

With a loud whooping and hollering and a frantic beating on pots and pans, the Friends entered the woods. Maggie and Martha Jo split up, with Martha Jo following a line close to the creek and Maggie plunging straight into the heart of the woods.

Birds and squirrels, startled by the clamor, took flight before the noisy brigade. As the rain drizzled down, drops of moisture clung to the tree branches and froze in a thin, glistening sheet.

Maggie pulled her toboggan cap low over her eyes and walked swiftly to generate all the body heat she could. The banging noise from her pot joined the loud din that was echoing through the woods.

She came unexpectedly upon a white-tail buck, poised in indecision under an ancient oak tree. Out of the corner of her eye she glimpsed the barrel of a rifle being lifted into position.

"Shoo! Get out of here," she yelled as she beat frantically on her pot. The buck leaped high into the air and bounded into a thicket. Maggie continued the clamor on her pot until she was sure the buck was safely away.

"Where's your horn, Maggie?" Adam Trent stepped out of his deer stand.

She whirled to face him. "How did you know who it was?" To her mortification he looked every bit as good as he had looked Wednesday. His fleece-lined buckskin coat lent him the devastatingly virile look of a man out to conquer the wilderness.

"You're like a bad penny, Maggie. You keep turning up." His debonair smile took some of the bite out of the words.

"You bet your buckskin britches I keep turning up. As long as you persist in this wholesale slaughter of animals, I'll be there."

"That's an unfortunate choice of words."

"But accurate."

"Hardly. I'd say misinformed, to put it kindly."

"Oh, please spare me your kindness. A girl could get hurt by the brand of kindness that's backed by a forty-four magnum." She inclined her head to indicate the gun in Adam's hand. A look of surprise crossed his face that she had accurately named the kind of gun he was carrying. "I'm not quite as misinformed as you'd like to believe."

"In some areas you are, Maggie." He paused and pinned her to the spot with his vivid blue eyes. "And I've decided to educate you."

Maggie's green eyes snapped at him, and she bristled like an angry cat. "I don't need educating by any animal assassin." Taking a firm hold on her pot and spoon, she stalked toward him. "Move out of my way. I have work to do."

His hand snaked out and caught her by the arm. Drawing her up close, he studied the stubborn, angry expression on her face. "So much passion and fire," he murmured.

Maggie reeled under the impact of his stare. She felt herself drowning in the intensity of his gaze, a willing victim going under for the third time and loving every minute of it.

"I wonder what you would be like if all that passion were turned in a different direction." As he spoke the words, his face moved closer and closer toward hers, until she felt the heat of his breath stirring a lock of hair that had escaped her cap.

With superhuman effort she mentally pulled herself away from the hypnotic effect of those eyes. "You'll never know. Barbarian!"

His head swooped down with the swiftness of a night hawk, and his lips took possession of hers. Chilled by the December wind, his lips crushed fiercely against hers, demanding a response. His strong arms pulled her close against his body, and even through all the layers of clothes they wore she could feel its muscled strength.

Warmed by his kiss, her cold lips opened and moved beneath his, slowly, sensuously at first, and then in a fever of undisguised passion. His hand came up under her jacket as his tongue plunged home in the soft, warm caverns of her mouth. She met the rapier thrusts of his tongue with soft animal cries of desire.

A burning heat blossomed in her loins and spread slowly throughout her body, threatening to consume her. Locked together in the silent depths of the woods, their lips searched, demanded, explored.

Maggie knew she was courting danger. But she clung to him a while longer, skirting the edge of the chasm, unwilling to plunge over the edge and unable to pull back. His lips felt wonderful on hers, and she selfishly wanted to enjoy them a moment longer, knowing that this could not, must not, happen again.

Adam's hands moved under her jacket, seeking the silken swell of her breasts. "No," she whispered hoarsely. "Let me go." She shoved against him with all her strength, breaking the passionate spell they had woven. Her hand shook as she brought her soup spoon up into the air and held it in a threatening position. "I'm going to clobber you if you don't move out of my way."

"Tigress," he said with a growl. "You don't need educating; you need taming." He stood squarely in her path, an immovable hunk of maleness; challenging her, mocking her.

"I don't need anything from you." Her lips still felt pouty and warm from his kiss. She had a hard time shaping them around the angry words. She brandished the spoon. "Move!"

"I liked you better with the horn." His hand shot out and grasped her wrist, stilling the threatening motion. "You're a fascinating wildcat, Maggie, and I intend to tame you." He moved a step closer to her, closing the distance she had deliberately put between them.

She was suffocating. She took a deep breath, drawing fresh air into her lungs. "What do you intend to do? Mount me and hang me on your wall?"

A slow grin spread across his face. "Mount you?" he asked softly. "Now there's an interesting idea."

"Savage!"

His deep, rich laugh filled the ice-bound woods. "Fight, my lithe, baggy-britched tigress."

"You leave my britches out of this!" she yelled. The heat in her body had spread to her brain. She couldn't even think straight with him towering over her, raking her with his incredible blue eyes.

"Gladly. I'm anxious to see if you're hiding a woman's body under them."

"You're an animal. A beast!" she snapped.

"Why, Maggie, I thought you loved animals."

"Stop twisting everything I say!" she yelled.

"You're the one who came to the woods armed for battle." His hand came up and cupped her cold face. He leaned over, bringing his lips dangerously close to hers. "What's the matter, Tigress? Don't you know how to be a gracious victor?"

"I won again today. Just remember that." He was so close now, she could see a tiny V-shaped scar on his jawline.

"Did you, Maggie?" he asked softly as his lips descended on hers once more. She closed her eyes under the onslaught as he took her mouth with maddening ease.

Maggie sent an agonized prayer winging heavenward as she felt herself being captured by Adam's embrace. Even as her lips moved hungrily under his, she knew that he was trying to sidetrack her with his sensuous tactics. Oh, Lord, she groaned silently. Just for a moment longer would she feast on this forbidden nectar.

When she thought that she could stand the exquisite agony no longer, when she thought the entire world was going to crash at her feet and splinter into a thousand icy pieces, Adam's lips left hers.

He broke the kiss and stepped back from her. "Did you?" he challenged. Turning away from her, he walked swiftly into the woods, leaving her with a dangling spoon, a silent pot, and a thundering heart.

She lifted her hand and thunked the spoon listlessly against the pot. The dull sound of metal against metal echoed in the strangely silent woods. Maggie sniffed loudly and place her gloved hands over her cold nose. Had everybody else already gone home? She cocked her ears, listening. The woods echoed with a mocking silence.

Walking carefully, as if she might shatter, Maggie made her way back to the pickup truck. All the other vehicles were gone, and there was no sign of Martha Jo. Maggie opened the truck door to crawl inside and spied a note on the seat. "Maggie. I've hitched a ride with Carl. What took you so long? Martha Jo."

Automatically Maggie turned the key in the ignition and sat unmoving, letting the truck warm up. The sound was loud in the early-morning stillness.

She stretched her cold hands and feet toward the heater, letting the warmth seep into her. What was she going to do? she wondered. She was a shambles from her encounter with Adam. Easing the truck into gear, she pulled onto the road. She couldn't help herself; she was fascinated by the man. It was the same kind of fascination that compelled a child to reach toward a hot stove. And she would be burned. She had no doubt of that. He was the antithesis of all she believed in. He was a sportsman, a hunter, while she was an animal lover, a preservationist.

Without thinking, Maggie turned her truck onto Highway 371, driving toward her childhood home. Sheer habit took over. Whenever Maggie had a problem that was too big for her, she turned to her father. Dr. Merriweather had always been a rock in all the storms that had raged around Maggie.

Maggie parked her truck under the huge magnolia tree in front of the modest brick house. She hopped out and headed toward the back of the house, to the concrete-block building that housed the veterinary clinic. Dr. Merriweather always fed the animals at this time of day.

She opened the door and just stood there for a minute, smelling the familiar antiseptic odors, feeling the comforting security of being home.

Dr. Merriweather was bending over a sick beagle, coaxing him to eat. "Come on, boy. Just one little bite." His thick white hair was in disarray from his habit of constantly raking his fingers through it. A baggy gray sweater, its pockets stuffed with lollipops, hung on his spare frame.

Maggie's heart lifted at the sight of him. "Dad?" she called softly.

He swiveled his shaggy head toward the sound, and his weathered face crinkled into a smile. "Maggie, darlin', how good to see you." He came forward and wrapped her in a warm embrace. "Come over here and take a look at Joe. He's pining away for his litter mate, poor little fellow. They both had distemper, and the other one died yesterday. See if you can do anything for the little guy." As Dr. Merriweather talked, a sense of peace stole over her. The gentleness and compassion that radiated from her father enveloped her, stilling the turmoil in her mind.

Together they bent over the tiny black-and-tan spotted beagle and encouraged him to eat. Their efforts were finally rewarded when his pink tongue came out and he began to lap up the soupy mixture that had been prepared for him.

Dr. Merriweather beamed. "You always did have a magic touch with the animals." He straightened and pushed his glasses back on his nose. "How about some tea, darlin'?"

She matched her stride to his as they left the clinic and went through the back door into Dr. Merriweather's old-fashioned kitchen. A fire crackled cheerily in the small stone fireplace, and two rockers with blue chintz cushions stood nearby.

Maggie pulled off her coat and hat, sat in one of the rockers, and leaned forward, holding her hands close to the fire. "I've come for tea and sympathy, Dad."

"That's what I figured." He puttered about the kitchen, whistling as he set the tea kettle on to boil. "I'm here, Maggie."

That was all he said. She knew he would never pry but would wait for Maggie to confide as little or as much as she wished.

"You know about Friends of the Animals?" The blazing fire cast a reddish glow over Maggie's tumbled hair. She had set the chair in motion and was rocking back and forth. The gentle rhythm, the crackling fire, and her father's presence began to lull her into a sense of well-being.

Dr. Merriweather came over to her carrying two cups of steaming tea. Placing one in Maggie's hand, he settled comfortably into the other rocker with his tea. "Yes. I'm proud of you for founding that organization. I've devoted my life to the care and welfare of animals. It's good to have my daughter following in my footsteps."

"We're trying to save game animals now by going into the woods and scaring them away with noise."

Dr. Merriweather chuckled. "A bit unorthodox but probably very effective."

Maggie smiled. "I think so." She paused, biting her lower lip. She hadn't come to talk about methods of saving the animals. That wasn't what was uppermost in her mind. She took a sip of her tea.

32 • PEGGY WEBB

"Dad, there's some high-powered opposition to my cause. Do you know Adam Trent?"

"Yes. He's very successful and influential, but underneath it all he's just a man, darlin', just like the rest of us."

"That means he has feet of clay, too, huh?" Her father nodded, and she continued. "It's not that I'm afraid to fight him, it's just that he bothers me in a way I never expected."

"You have courage and brains, Maggie, a formidable combination."

"You're not just saying that because you're prejudiced, are you?" she asked, teasing.

"Can I help it if I raised the most beautiful, most brilliant daughter in all of Lee County?" His glasses had slid down on his nose again, and he gazed fondly over them at Maggie. "What I'm saying, love, is that I have confidence in you."

"I needed to hear you say that, Dad. It puts things in proper perspective for me. I'm not fighting *against* Adam, I'm fighting for the animals."

The clock on the mantel chimed the hour as Maggie and her father sipped their tea and rocked in comfortable silence. At last she rose from her chair, toasty-warm and glowing with self-confidence. "I'd better be going, Dad."

"Be careful on the roads, Maggie. That drizzle is probably freezing, and they'll be slick." Dr. Merriweather helped Maggie into her jacket.

"Don't worry about me. I'm in my trusty four-wheel-drive." She kissed her father on the cheek and waved good-bye.

Because of the condition of the roads, Maggie canceled her Friends meeting that evening. She showered, shampooed her hair, put on a comfortable blue fleece bathrobe, and curled up in front of her fire with a stack of papers to grade. She chuckled to herself as she corrected the second-grade sentences. "Everthang I dun fun" was not good grammar, but it was truly delightful philosophy.

When the doorbell rang she wondered who would be crazy enough to be out on the roads. The steady rain had not stopped all day, and the below-freezing temperatures had left the roads covered with a sheet of ice.

She wrapped her robe more snugly around herself, pulled the belt in tight, raked a hand through her still-damp mane of honey-gold curls, and went to answer the door. Adam Trent stood in the glow of her porch light.

"Is this where the Friends of the Animals group meets?"

"I canceled the meeting." She stood in the door and thought of the way he had kissed her in the woods. Her knees turned to butter. He had no business being here, she thought, none at all.

"May I come in or do you intend to make me stand out here and freeze?"

She certainly thought it would be best for all concerned if he stood on her porch and froze solid. Then she would be rid of him, and there would be no one to make her forget her cause. She meant to say coolly, "I really don't care," and march huffily back into her warm den, but instead it came out, "Come inside. Can I get you a cup of hot tea?" Sometimes Maggie's deeply ingrained Southern manners managed to prevent her from doing wicked deeds.

When Adam Trent stepped inside her cottage, it suddenly seemed small. There was hardly anywhere she could turn without brushing against his coat sleeve or rubbing against his legs. She thought of going around him by climbing over the back of the sofa but dismissed that as too obvious. "If you'll sit there"—she nodded in the general direction of a chair—"I'll go make the tea."

She saw her den for the first time as Adam's eyes

took it in—the antique rocker, the fat, comfy calico sofa, the braided throw rugs on the polished wooden floor. "Nice," he said.

She beamed all the way to the kitchen and felt as if she had been tapped for a *House and Garden* layout. She clattered around, knocking teacups and saucers about in the cabinet as she searched for a matching pair. Behind her, the copper teapot got up a full head of steam.

The two garage-sale cups in her hands looked almost the same. She put one in its saucer and had begun to lower the other when the teapot whistled. The cup clattered to the brick floor and shattered. "Oh, damn," she muttered.

She bent down to pick up the pieces and her robe gaped open, top and bottom, revealing a lovely length of leg and her soft, satiny cleavage.

"Need any help in here?" Adam Trent stood leaning against the doorframe, reviewing the scene. His eyes spent all of two seconds on the broken teacup, and then came to rest on Maggie.

"I was right. There's quite a woman underneath those baggy britches." His eyes gleamed in a predatory way, and his smile made Maggie think of a big, fat cat getting ready to swallow the canary.

Maggie jumped up amid the broken china and jerked her robe shut, belting it furiously. "Did you come all the way out here to Belden to leer at me? If you did, just get back into your Mercedes and go home." She clutched the robe high around her throat.

"I did not, but when opportunity knocks I always answer the call."

"That wasn't opportunity knocking; that was the teapot." She jerked the kettle off the stove and sloshed the hot water into the unbroken cup, then reached into the cabinet and chose another cup for herself. "I don't know why I'm even bothering to pour you any tea. You've worn out your welcome."

"It's good to know that for a while I was welcome." He walked up behind her and put his arms around her, steadying her hands with his. "You're going to burn yourself."

She had already burned herself. That afternoon in the woods. And her wounds were still smarting. Every inch of flesh on her back tingled as Adam pressed his solid chest against her, assisting her in pouring the tea.

Somehow the water ended up in the cup, but Adam still stood with his arms around Maggie. "We've finished," she announced in a hopeful voice.

"On the contrary. We've just begun." He took the brimming cup from Maggie's hands and turned nonchalantly around as if he had just made a remark about the weather.

His words whirled in Maggie's head as she turned slowly to face him. His eyebrows were raised quizzically above his stunning blue eyes, and he looked perfectly delicious standing in the middle of her kitchen. Unconsciously she pulled the neck of her robe tighter. She had already consorted with this clever enemy once today, and she was too smart to make the same mistake twice. "How do you want your tea? With just a touch of arsenic?"

His smile was lazy, like an animal feasting his eyes on his prey. "How about with a touch of tea?" He watched her uncomprehending expression in amusement. "I assume you did intend to put some instant tea in this hot water?"

"Naturally," she said breezily as she whirled back to the cabinet and puttered noisily among the shelves, searching for the instant tea. Her garage-sale cups and saucers clanked and rattled from the onslaught of her furious search. If Adam wouldn't stand so close back there, she thought, breathing down her neck, she might be able to find what she was looking for.

"I see it on the front of the second shelf," Adam offered helpfully.

"I know that," Maggie snapped. "I was just rearranging the dishes." She grabbed the jar and viciously unscrewed the lid. "One spoon or two?"

"Two." He was chuckling openly now.

Holding the instant-tea jar in front of her chest like a sacrificial offering, Maggie approached him. He watched as she hastily dumped tea into his cup. "You can do your own stirring." She already regretted her burst of Southern hospitality. "If you can control yourself, we'll move into the den with our tea." She'd probably regret that, too, she mused. Wonder-boy bankers with gorgeous legs could be dangerous in a cozy den. She studied his legs as they moved into the room. No doubt about it. Under the trim fit of his slacks, she could just tell that his legs were gorgeous.

Adam sat on the plump calico sofa and managed to look as if he belonged there. The fire crackled cozily as he sipped his tea and glanced around the room. "Tell me, Maggie. What do you do when you're not crashing through the woods banging pots and pans, or carting little old ladies around on field trips in freezing weather?"

"I take it you didn't like my concert today?" Maggie smiled over her teacup at him. She could afford to be charitable. After all, she had won again. And his eyelashes curved so nicely on his cheeks when he lowered his eyes to look down at the teacup.

"Do you always throw down the gauntlet at every opportunity?"

"Yes."

His astonishing blue eyes caught and held hers captive until she could hardly breathe. "Then I was right," he said softly. "You do need taming."

"You can just march your gorgeous legs right out the front door if you're going to say ridiculous things." Enemies should never be invited to tea, she realized with a wonderful flash of hindsight.

His mouth crinkled up at the corners, and he took a huge gulp of tea to strangle his mirth. Obviously, he guessed, Maggie didn't realize what she had said, for she sat sipping her tea and looking smug.

"Let's start this conversation over, Maggie. We're two adults. Surely we can be civil."

He shouldn't have smiled, she thought. It was an incredible smile that would melt icebergs and cold hearts. If he hadn't smiled, she could have turned him out into the wintry night and let him freeze his gorgeous legs. Her eyes gleamed at him over the teacup as she said, "Try me."

"What do you do?"

"I teach second grade at East Heights Elementary."

"Lucky little rascals. My second-grade teacher looked like a female version of Frankenstein."

"I'm sure she wasn't that bad."

"Yes, she was. I distinctly remember a wart on her chin." He placed his empty teacup on the table beside the sofa and moved toward the fire. Maggie shifted uncomfortably in the antique rocking chair and wished he would sit back down. Civil was one thing; shockingly close was another altogether. Adam leaned an elbow on the mantel above her crackling fire. "Do you approach teaching with the same spirit you use in your FOA activities?"

"Certainly. Dad taught us to give one hundred percent to whatever we do."

"Us?"

"My brother Jim and me. Mom died when I was five, and Dad threw all the books away in raising us. We were as wild as two buck Indians, and the whole community said we would never amount to a hill of beans. Dad just smiled and went quietly about his business of healing sick animals and caring for us. He taught us to be free-thinking, independent, and outspoken."

Adam smiled. "I'll vouch for that." He leaned close to Maggie and scrutinized her face. "I should have known. Your eyes are the same."

"You know my brother?"

"Jim Merriweather is a customer of mine. I gave him the loan to start his farm when every other banker in town said he was too young, too much of a risk. He was filled with the same fire that I see in you when you defend animals."

"They deserve to be defended with fire—and brimstone, too, if necessary. Every living creature has the right to live, to be free." Passion for her cause burned brightly within her, and she sprang from her chair, unable to sit still as she spoke her staunch beliefs. "I watched sick animals come into Dad's clinic, and I saw their struggles to live. I was there, Adam. Animals are capable of feelings, of showing love. They don't deserve to be slaughtered."

"Hunting is not slaughter, Maggie."

"Oh, no?" Maggie put her hands on her hips and charged forward for the cause. "Then, why do you carry such a big gun?"

Adam reached out, grasped her wrists in his hands, and pulled her toward him. "Maggie. Maggie." His voice was low and urgent. "Why are you so stubborn . . . and so damned beautiful?"

It couldn't be December, with ice on the roads, Maggie thought. It was much too hot in her den. Oh, why did this enemy have to be so pure-male-animal stunning? She pulled fiercely, trying to release her wrists from his grasp. "Why are you here, Adam?"

"I came to your FOA meeting."

"To steal our battle plans?"

"I told you this afternoon. I plan to educate you." He pulled her a fraction of an inch closer. She could see a small muscle pulsing in his cheek. "I've decided to invest some time in you, Maggie. You challenge me. Intrigue me."

She summoned up a remnant of bravado from the depths of her soul. "You're wasting your time. I'm not one of your banks."

"How well I know." His eyes were blue fire that threatened to consume her. "But I'm going to tame you, Maggie." He was so close now that she could feel the heat of his breath stirring against her cheek.

She almost melted and ran down into her fuzzy slippers. "You're suffering from delusions. I don't consort with the enemy."

"And I don't walk away from a challenge." With quick sureness, his lips scorched down the side of her cheek and burned briefly across her lips.

"What are you doing?" she whispered hoarsely.

"Giving you something besides your cause to think about." He released her wrists, stepped back, and smiled at her. "That robe is quite an improvement over your baggy britches, Tigress." He walked toward the door and then turned back to her. "See you in the woods, Maggie."

The front door clicked shut behind him, and Maggie stood there clutching her burning face. In the stillness of the night, she heard his car door slam. The Mercedes engine purred into life, and gravel crunched under his tires as he spun out of her driveway.

Why couldn't life be as simple as it was in the days of Joan of Arc, when activists were merely burned at the stake? She touched her lips with her fingertips and gazed at her closed front door. "No!" she said fiercely. She would not think of Adam. With superhuman effort, she forced herself to remember what she was fighting for. "Barbarian," she muttered halfheartedly, then walked to the kitchen and picked up the broken pieces of her china teacup.

Four

The cold front kept its icy grip on Tupelo for three days, paralyzing the city. Snowplows were rare in the deep South, and tire chains were as scarce as icicles on the equator. Only the foolhardy ventured forth on the treacherous roads. The wise accepted the rare, ice-bound days as a gift of leisure time, perfectly suited to the slow pace of the region.

She was not being foolhardy, Maggie told herself as she shoved her belly-dancing costume into a tote bag and slipped her parka on over her army pants. Just . . . adventurous. She and Martha Jo had enrolled in a belly-dancing class back in September, a night class taught through the Parks and Recreation Department, and their teacher had said that they could come in any time and practice with the records.

Not that she would ever make any sultan sit up and take notice, Maggie mused as she carefully eased her pickup truck onto the icy roads. Belly-dancing was just a fun thing to do, and dancing in a costume of gauze and bangles during a freezing spell appealed to Maggie's sense of the ridiculous.

She whistled a snatch of *Scheherezade* and tried to remember how to keep the ruby from falling out of her navel. The truck skidded. Well, heck, if she slid into a ditch, somebody would come along and pull her out. The back end of the truck righted itself then, and Maggie inched across the bridge to Bel Air Center. The Highway Department had spread a layer of salt and slag on the bridge, so that she felt safe as she chugged across. Except for a solitary bakery truck, Maggie had the road all to herself.

She slid down the hill to the parking lot and noticed with surprise that several cars were already there. Maybe there was a party going on, she thought, and she could join the fun. She hopped from the truck, grabbed her tote bag, pulled her toboggan cap low over her forehead, and walked inside the Center. Its cavernous hall was empty except for a lone man sitting half-asleep in a chair in front of the ballroom. Maggie tiptoed in his direction, hoping not to disturb him when she entered. Her class was always held in the ballroom, and that was where the records were kept.

The man snorted and shook his shaggy head as she approached. He grabbed his fat stomach with two chubby hands and peered nearsightedly up at her. The dark circles under his eyes and his heavy jowls gave him the look of a panda bear.

"Where you goin', young feller?" The two front legs of the straight-backed chair he was sitting in banged against the wooden floor. "This ain't no Boy Scout meetin'."

"I'm not a boy . . ." The man glared distrustfully at her. ". . . scout," she finished lamely. She realized that all her hair was tucked up under her cap.

The panda-bear man ignored her statement. "They's a meetin' goin' on in there, and I had to come all the way out here in the ice to lock up and clean up after them." He scratched his shaggy head. "They just ain't no accountin' for what foolish folks will do these days. Makin' a feller go out in weather like this! The whole world's gone plumb loco. Ain't that right, young feller?"

Telling the man again that she was not a boy

would be futile, Maggie decided. "I'll just slip in quietly and get my records and—"

"Can't let you do that, young feller." The man shifted his rotund body so that one leg was blocking the doorway. "They don't want no commotion. Them fellers in there is sure 'nuff aristicats."

Maggie put her hands on her hips and rocked back on her heels. "Aristicats," were they? Well, there was nothing she liked better than giving a few pompous "aristicats" a run for their money. Yessir, she'd just shake them up a little. There was too much stuffiness and not enough fun in the world.

"Thank you, sir," she told the guardian of the "aristicats" in a meek voice. "I'll just be on my way." She whirled quickly before the man could see her broad grin.

Her heels tapped smartly on the floor as she strode with purpose toward the ladies' rest room. Once inside, she shed her heavy winter clothes and donned the flimsy belly-dancing costume. The gold gossamer skirt hung low around her hips, suspended there from a wide band of gold sequins and spangles. The skimpy gold-sequined bra with its tiny straps looked as if a puff of wind might blow it away. Maggie twirled around, her golden hair and the golden skirt making a bright cloud around her. She laughed aloud. This was going to be fun.

And now for the coup de grâce, she thought happily. Maggie reached into her bag and brought out a large imitation ruby. She fitted it carefully into her navel and hoped that she remembered how to hold her stomach muscles taut, so that it would stay there.

Fastening on her finger cymbals, she backed out the bathroom door, butting it open with her fanny, and strode back down the hall. When she neared panda bear, she slowed down and put a flirtatious sway in her walk.

Panda bear's eyes nearly popped out of his head. He stood up so hastily that his chair fell with a clunk to the floor. "Well, I'll be a son of a gun! Where'd you come from?"

Maggie nodded toward the bathroom door and shot him a dazzling smile that made his Adam's apple bob up and down. "I'm the entertainment," she said sweetly.

"They didn't mention no entertainment."

"I'm sure it must have been an oversight."

"Lordy mercy! I'm sure it was." He spoke directly to Maggie's cleavage. His eyes swiveled slowly downward, taking in the ruby and the spangled band around her hips. "You got quite a hitch in your git along there."

"Why, thank you." I think, she added to herself. "Would you mind holding the door open for me?"

"Would I mind . . ." His Adam's apple did another jig as his eyes moved back to Maggie's face. "The door? Lordy mercy, the door! 'Course not." He tripped over the fallen chair and banged his foot against the wall, getting to the door.

Maggie lifted her arms, clicked her finger cymbals, and backed into the room, hips swaying to the remembered beat of the music from *Scheherazade*. The sudden silence that greeted her entry was electrifying. She smiled as she danced, seeing the open-mouthed amazement on the faces of the six men seated at a corner table. They were "aristicats," all right. To a man, their hair was carefully styled, and their dark ties were knotted under crisp white shirts. They looked as if they had just stepped from the pages of *Esquire*, Maggie decided, and would never spill soup or smack bubble gum or go to a belly-dancing performance.

Maggie swayed and swirled and clicked her cymbals, wondering if she'd regret this tomorrow. Sometimes her impulsive actions got her into more trouble than she cared to think about.

"What the hell is going on?" The roar was unmistakably Adam Trent's.

Maggie stopped dead in her tracks, her right hip still poised on the upbeat, not daring to turn around. And then all pandemonium broke loose.

"Where did that girl come from?"

"My Lord, she has a ruby in her . . ."

"Who hired her?"

"What kind of banking seminar is this, anyway?"

"You have to admit, George, that she has panache!"

Maggie slowly turned to face the music. Adam stood at the podium, one button on his beautifully tailored suit jacket unbuttoned and one perfectly polished shoe resting on the rail of a chair that was shoved under the table. His familiar blue eyes blazed over at her, and she couldn't tell if they were shining with anger or amusement.

Oh, help! she thought wildly. She'd crashed a banking seminar and Adam was the head "aristi-cat." There was nothing quite like the feeling of looking *after* you have leaped, and it was a feeling all too familiar to Maggie. An extra shot of adrenaline pumped into her veins as she stared boldly back at Adam, hands on her hips and head held high.

"Is there a costume party and somebody forgot to tell me?" There was a general hubbub still going on in the room around them, but Maggie heard only Adam. His rich, deep voice made goose bumps pop up along her bare arms. She had forgotten how incredibly handsome he was. Well, almost.

"No. This is the dance-instruction room and somebody forgot to tell you."

One eyebrow inclined upward over his extraordinary eyes. "And you are the emissary, bringing the news?" He studied the golden girl in front of him, his eyes taking in the alluring curves and gorgeous legs visible beneath the gossamer skirt. "There's been quite an improvement in emissaries lately."

"I'm not an emissary; I'm just here to . . . to . . ." Maggie was not handling the situation with her usual aplomb, and that made her furious. "I'm here to dance," she finally got out.

"Be my guest." Adam still stood at the podium, one foot resting casually on the chair rail, completely dignified and utterly in charge.

"Suddenly I don't like the audience." Maggie thrust out her chin and tried to keep from shivering. The costume was awfully skimpy, and it was dreadfully cold outside. Or was her trembling caused by the blaze in Adam's eyes as they traveled boldly up and down her body? she wondered. He made no attempt to hide his fascination with the beautiful woman standing before him.

"Correct me if I'm wrong. It was you who chose the audience."

Damn! she fumed. He certainly didn't make things easy. But then, he never had. Her mind reeled backward to the night in her den, the night he had repeated his intent to tame her. Could he? Green eyes locked with blue. Impossible! Or was it?

"Yes, I did," she agreed quietly. She flung her hair back and glanced around the room. How long had it been since any of those men had done a single impulsive thing? she thought. How long since they had laughed with abandon? How long since they had had fun just for the heck of it? Maggie's hips began to sway, and an impish grin lit her face. "I certainly did," she added with renewed confidence.

Adam's eyes widened in disbelief. "Maggie, what the hell are you doing?" he hissed.

"Dancing." She grinned. "Taking a little starch out of some stuffed shirts."

"Stuffed shirts!" he exploded. "Maggie, stop that."

"Loosen up, Adam. Have a little fun." She danced across to him, her hips undulating in the fascinating rhythm of the East. Leaning close, she clicked the finger cymbals in his face. "Or better still, go outside and check your Mercedes while I finish my number. I skidded down the hill, and I may have rearranged a fender or two."

Adam cast a beseeching look toward the ceiling and turned his back on Maggie. He banged the gavel sharply on the podium and had to bang it once more before her delighted audience would give him their attention. "We'll take a coffee break while I clear up this . . . situation." The pause in his words was barely noticeable.

Was the head "aristicat" rattled? Maggie grinned. Tame her, would he? She weaved around behind him and bumped him lightly with her hip.

He made a strangled sound into the microphone and then resumed speaking. "Coffee is set up in the adjoining room. I'll see everybody back here in fifteen minutes." He banged the gavel with unnecessary vigor as a sign of dismissal.

"Aw, hell, Trent, you've spoiled all the fun."

"I was just beginning to enjoy the show."

"I don't know who planned it, but it's the best bank seminar I've attended all year."

With good-natured joshing, the group of bankers left the ballroom, and Maggie and Adam were all alone. He turned to face her in the quiet room, and her hips slowed, faltered, swayed once more, and then stopped.

Adam's eyes were riveted on hers, and somehow the dance had stopped being just fun and had become an erotic ritual, the slave girl entertaining the sheikh.

"Don't stop now. You have my undivided attention." His voice was soft, seductive, and exceedingly intimate.

Maggie's breath caught in her throat and her ruby popped to the floor. What had happened to fun and frolic? They were playing a new game now, and only Adam knew all the rules. His eyes consumed her, and she felt like a golden butterfly trapped in a bright blue flame.

Swiftly she bent down to retrieve her ruby, her skirts fanning out around her on the polished wooden floor. Adam was quicker. He knelt down, scooped up the imitation jewel, and held it just out of her reach. "Is this what you're looking for?"

He was kneeling so close beside her that she could feel the scratch of his wool-clad thigh against her thinly clad legs. "Yes." She reached up to take the ruby, and he caught her arm with his free hand.

The heat of his touch on her bare arm spread through her body and licked little flames along her nerve endings. For a small eternity their eyes caught and held, and then he turned his gaze to the ruby. "It's still warm from your flesh."

She shivered in spite of the flame that was now burning boldly through her body. Her legs felt loose and rubbery. If she could get them to move, she thought desperately, she'd grab her ruby and run.

Adam turned the ruby in his hand. "It's fascinating. When I turn it this way, the light catches one side and I think I've seen all its sparkle. But when I turn it this way, an entirely new facet is revealed. I wonder if I could ever discover all there is to know about this jewel?"

The blue fire of his eyes devoured her once more, and she knew Adam wasn't talking about rubies. "It's not real." Her voice was barely a whisper in the huge, empty room.

"Isn't it?" Adam asked softly. "From where I sit,

it is." His eyes caught her up and carried her into a new dimension. "I'm bewitched."

She looked at the lock of hair hanging boyishly across his forehead, at the soft down of the skin across his handsome cheekbones, and the dark beard shadow on his square jaw. He was mistaken. She was the one bewitched. And if she didn't move her legs soon, she would be so completely under Adam Trent's spell that there would be no escape. "I need to go. Your friends will soon be back."

Her words didn't have the impact she'd thought they would. She half expected him to become all spit and polish again, the proper "aristicat."

He bent so close that his breath stirred the soft tendrils of hair around her cheeks. "Then, Maggie, my tigress"—his words caressed her name and possessively emphasized her new title—"I suggest you hurry. I'm not partial to sharing."

He placed the fake ruby into her trembling hand and closed her numb fingers over the jewel. Bending his head, he kissed her closed fist, a warm, lingering kiss that melted Maggie all the way down to her gold-polished toes.

Together they stood up. His hands grasped her bare shoulders, the fingers pressing warmly into her flesh. Her lips parted, and she waited for the kiss she knew would come, the kiss she dreaded and the kiss she desired.

But Adam released her and stood with his gaze burning over her face.

Maggie spun around and hurried from the room. Behind her, she could hear the sounds of the bankers reentering the room. She whirled past the open-mouthed panda-bear doorkeeper and rushed into the ladies' room. She leaned, panting, against the tile wall, marveling that she was still in one piece. With shaking hands, she changed her clothes and walked out into the cold December evening. All the way home she wondered just who had "won" this latest encounter, and why.

In a fit of indignation she flung her belly-dancing costume into a corner of the closet, then marched to her kitchen to make a huge popper of corn. She carried the overflowing bowl of popcorn to her den and shared the fluffy white grains with her three dogs. The impatient thumps of Frisky's tail told her that she was getting more than her share, but Maggie didn't care. She stuffed the delicious morsels into her mouth and brooded. It would serve Adam Trent right, she thought, if she got so fat she couldn't ever fit into that wretched belly-dancing costume again.

Maggie was in a general snit. For two days she stomped and fumed around her house in such uncharacteristic ill humor that even her dogs gave her a wide berth. She kept telling herself that Adam Trent had nothing to do with her mood, but at odd moments she would find herself thinking about his incredible eyes and the way his hair fell across his forehead. She got so mad at him for intruding on her thoughts that she fervently hoped he had to go to another meeting of "aristicats" and that he froze his tail off en route.

The capricious sun that had hidden its face from the South for three days beamed down with a vengeance on Tuesday, melting all the ice and restoring activity to the town.

After an unexpected holiday, Maggie's second-graders were buoyed up with energy and enthusiasm. She breathed a sigh of relief when they went off to the library and gave her a much-needed break. Even the stiff cushions of the sofa in the teachers' lounge felt good as she collapsed on them.

"If the Lord will just let me live till Christmas vacation, next week, I'll probably give up cussing."

Martha Jo sank onto the cushion beside Maggie and kicked off her shoes.

Maggie grunted in assent. "That'll be the day."

"I take it you haven't seen today's paper." Martha Jo reached into the box on the coffee table in front of them and grabbed a chocolate doughnut.

"I haven't had time. What does today's paper have to do with Christmas vacation? The school board hasn't changed the dates, has it?"

Martha Jo rose and crossed the lounge to retrieve the newspaper that was lying on top of the copy machine. Flipping it open to page two, she began to read: " 'Prominent Tupelo Citizen Blasts FOA. Adam Trent, president of Mutual Bank, leveled some high-powered criticism against the Friends of the Animals.' "

Maggie was on her feet, breathing fire, her exhaustion forgotten. "Let me see that." She grabbed the newspaper and scanned the article rapidly. " 'Calling the group uninformed . . .' Uninformed indeed! The barbarian! '. . . and stating that the goal they hope to achieve is the same as that of honorable sportsmen . . .' Ha! There's no honor among assassins. '. . . he suggested a summit meeting between himself and the group's volatile leader, Maggie Merriweather.' I'll just bet he did. Well, I'll show him volatile! 'Citing their childish tactics as an example . . .' Wait till I get my hands on him!" Maggie flung the paper down and stomped around the small teachers' lounge.

Martha Jo watched her with amused admiration. "*That's* why I surmised that you had not seen the paper. The magnificent Mr. Trent dealt us quite a blow, didn't he?"

"It's not even a glancing one. I don't care how many interviews the prominent Mr. Trent gives, he will not stop us." Maggie's feet, in black leather boots, tapped the floor angrily, and her sapphire-blue wool skirt swished about her legs as she marched up and down, plotting. Suddenly she grinned and plopped down on the sofa. The grin became a satisfied chuckle.

"It must be good. What diabolical plan have you hatched against the magnificent enemy?" Martha Jo licked the chocolate icing off her fingers and reached for another doughnut. "You really should try these, Maggie. Mrs. Samuelson made them for us." She held one up to her friend.

Maggie took the doughnut and absently laid it on top of her purse. "If Adam Trent is impressed with our 'childish tactics' now, just wait till I finish with him this afternoon. He'll have to call a special press conference just to spread the word."

"If you're not going to eat that doughnut, give it back to me." Martha Jo bit off a generous mouthful. "If I didn't have a scout meeting this afternoon, I'd go with you." She leaned back against the sofa. "What a magnificent hunk."

"The doughnut?" Maggie grinned at her.

"No, you goose. The man." Martha Jo sighed dramatically. "Or haven't you noticed?" She narrowed her eyes and looked closely at Maggie.

Maggie turned from the close scrutiny and began gathering up her class's papers. Land, though, hadn't she noticed! She'd worked herself up into a sweat trying to imagine what Adam Trent's bare chest looked like. Not to mention his gorgeous legs. "The bell's going to ring." She rattled her papers and wished the bell would rescue her. She wasn't ready to admit to her friend that not only had she noticed what a magnificent hunk the enemy was, but that she had also consorted with him shamelessly.

"You *have* noticed! I want to hear every juicy detail."

"The bell's ringing." Maggie snatched up her papers and flew out the door of the lounge.

Martha Jo's voice echoed down the hall after her. "We'll discuss this later."

Maggie helped her twenty-two chattering second-graders bundle into warm coats and hats and answered dozens of questions about the next week's Christmas party. When the dismissal bell finally rang, she waved them all out the door.

She jumped into her pickup truck and hurried home on the bypass. Intent on her errand, she gave her pets a hasty greeting and rushed inside for her trumpet. Slinging the case onto the seat next to her, she roared back down her driveway and headed into Tupelo, straight toward Mutual Bank.

Christmas shoppers crowded the city streets, and Maggie had to circle the block three times before she could find a parking space in front of the downtown bank. Working quickly, she unsnapped her trumpet case and took out her silver horn. "So, you like a challenge, do you, Adam Trent?" she muttered as she worked. "Well, today you're going to get more than you bargained for."

Letting her trumpet dangle from her hand, she entered the bank through the revolving glass doors and walked through the crowd, scouting the place. She was looking for the perfect spot, a central space for the grandstand play she had in mind. Adam had asked for a summit meeting; well, he was going to get it.

A row of tellers' windows lined one side of Mutual Bank, and a row of polished desks, occupied by discreet-looking women, lined the opposite side. Smack in the middle of all the polished brass and shining glass and judicious efficiency stood an oak table just waiting for Maggie and her trumpet.

Grinning wickedly, she swung herself atop the table with hardly any trouble at all. Only a few people noticed her ascent, and they turned their heads quickly aside. Maggie stood up on the tabletop, planted her feet firmly apart, and lifted the trumpet to her lips. The brazen notes blasted forth in the staid old bank. Da, da, da, dum, de, dah. "Charge!" Maggie yelled.

One bank teller dropped a roll of quarters, and another frantically pressed her foot on the alarm button. An excited crowd gathered around Maggie as quarters clanked across the polished floor and alarm bells clanged throughout the bank.

A door banged open on the mezzanine, and Adam Trent barreled out of the president's office. Leaning over the balcony, he viewed the mass confusion in his usually sedate bank. He quickly spotted the source of the trouble, towering atop his check-writing tablé like a beautiful avenging goddess. "Maggie!" he yelled. "Get down from there."

Maggie smiled with pleasure. She had enticed the lion from his lair. Lifting the trumpet to her lips, again she played the cavalry charge. The milling crowd looked up at the enraged man on the balcony and back at the gleeful woman on the table. Excitement mounted as the audience began to speculate about the unusual and chaotic situation.

"Dammit, Maggie! Stop that."

"You wanted a summit conference, Adam. I've just called the meeting to order."

"Order, hell. Get off that table."

"Why? The whole world already knows about my 'childish tactics.' It was right there in the newspaper, in black and white."

"Maggie," he said, warning her. The bank alarm still sounded, and people in the chattering crowd were taking bets on who would win the argument. Piped-in Christmas music played on beneath all the hubbub. "Will somebody turn off that damned alarm?" Adam yelled in the direction of his office. Abruptly, the clanging stopped. With long, angry strides Adam crossed the mezzanine to the executive elevator. He was whisked downstairs, where he emerged like a stalking beast going in for the kill. The crowd parted before him.

Maggie watched him coming. The sheer physical impact of him—the powerfully built body, the magnificent eyes, the firm, square jaw—hit her in the stomach, and she almost began to regret what she was doing to him. It was too late to back out now, though; she was already committed to her maverick ways of confronting him.

With grudging admiration Maggie observed him as Adam assumed a smooth, professional manner the minute he met the public. He was in perfect control as he turned to greet them, to shake their hands, to assure them that he would take care of the matter at hand. His progress toward her was impeded by excited customers, but not once did he deviate from his target.

He was so close now that Maggie could see the tiny flecks of blue in his tweed jacket. She took a deep breath and steadied her horn against her lips once more. It was time to attack. With her lips pressed tightly against the mouthpiece, she played "Taps."

Adam's face was grim as he looked up at her. "We have piped-in music here, Maggie. You'll have to take your live show somewhere else."

"It's not a show; it's a statement. Friends of the Animals intend to bury hunters."

Adam heaved a resigned sigh. "Somehow I'd rather you were marching on my lawn with signs."

"That's not my style."

"How well I know!" Adam let his eyes travel slowly over the woman standing proudly on top of his oak table. He took in the tousled mane of honey-colored hair, the stunning cat's eyes, the full, sensuous lips, and the alluring curves of her body under the soft angora sweater and swirling wool skirt. A glimpse of slender leg showed between the bottom of her skirt and the top of her black leather boots. She certainly did add spice to his antiseptic bank, he thought appreciatively.

A small grin played around the corners of his mouth. "I don't suppose I could interest you in coming down quietly, like a good little girl."

The smile was not lost on Maggie. She'd have to be careful, she reminded herself, or Adam Trent's charm would make her forget her purpose. "The 'volatile' leader of FOA?" She lifted her eyebrows. "Never. You've had your say; now I'll have mine."

"Maggie, about that newspaper story—"

"Yes. About that newspaper story, Adam Trent. Ordinary schoolteachers aren't sought out for interviews as often as prominent bankers, but, as you can see, we have our little ways of making our viewpoints known."

"Do you have to stand up there?" His grin grew wider. "Not that I'm complaining. The view from down here is fascinating. Not to mention educational."

Maggie was nonplussed for a moment. She glanced quickly down at her skirt to assure herself that it was long enough to cover the subject without being too educational. After all, she had intended to *pulverize* Adam Trent, not entertain him. "Surely a man of your prominence in the community has better things to do than gawk at me. Don't you have a helpless animal or two that you could be killing?"

With a swiftness that took her breath away, Adam reached up and grabbed her around the waist. He swung her down with ease and casually flung her across his shoulder. Her head and arms dangled helplessly down his back, and her legs were imprisoned across his chest. He sauntered back across the main floor of the bank, holding her like a sack of potatoes. And, to her mortification, he even stopped to talk to his customers on the way.

"Did Alfred take care of that Christmas loan you wanted, Mrs. Richmond?"

"He certainly did, Mr. Trent. My, my! This has been an interesting day." Mrs. Richmond adjusted her wool scarf and peered through her bifocals at Maggie. "Who is she, Mr. Trent? Somebody you hired to put on a show?"

Adam laughed. "She did liven things up a bit, didn't she, Mrs. Richmond?"

Behind his back, Maggie protested by smacking his backside with her horn.

"Ouch!"

Mrs. Richmond craned her neck so she could look up at her handsome banker. "What was that, Mr. Trent?"

"I said, 'Have a happy holiday,' Mrs. Richmond."

"Liar," Maggie muttered.

Adam gave her a tweak on the bottom. "Behave, Maggie." They continued their progress toward the elevator.

"Good thing Mrs. Richmond didn't see that. Monster." She attempted to put fire in her voice and failed miserably. Somewhere between "Taps" and Mrs. Richmond, she had gone from noble activist to absolute putty, she thought. It must have been about the same time her stomach impacted with Adam's broad shoulder. She contemplated his muscled thighs as she dangled upside down across his back. Why did Adam Trent have to be so butterflies-in-the-stomach magnificent?

The elevator door slid open. Adam stepped inside with his shapely burden and pressed the button for the executive floor.

"Put me down," Maggie commanded.

Adam's right arm tightened around her legs, and his left hand reached up to pat her on the bottom.

"You're the one who came for a summit conference, Maggie. Don't tell me you're ready to leave yet."

Maggie swallowed the dryness in her mouth. She admitted it—she was ready to run like a scared rabbit. Adam Trent had set her on fire, but not for her cause. "Of course not," she lied bravely. "I'm ready for you to put me down so that I can see your face when you explain those absurd accusations you made to that newspaper reporter."

"Maggie, that didn't happen the way you think it did."

"How do you know what I think?" She tried to squirm off his shoulder. "Put me down!"

"So you can blast that horn in my face?" He put both hands on her legs to hold her still. She thought she might faint. Maggie Merriweather, who rarely blushed and never fainted, actually considered going into a Victorian swoon in Adam Trent's arms. "No, thanks," he said crisply. "Not until you hear what I have to say."

The elevator door opened, but nobody paid it any attention, so it clicked shut again.

"Bucky Westing from the paper called me last night. He had heard about the encounter in Boguefala Bottom between the hunters and the FOA. Knowing that I am a hunter, he called me."

"I don't care who did the calling. *You* are the one who called us 'uninformed' and 'childish.'"

"The article served its purpose, didn't it, Maggie?"

Maggie was clearly at a disadvantage. Hanging across Adam's shoulder with the blood pounding in her ears and his hands burning her legs was no way to win this battle. "What purpose, you barbarian?"

Adam chuckled. "You're here, aren't you? I knew that giving that interview would be like waving a red flag before a bull. It was a surefire way of getting you to come here. We have some talking to do."

"I still say that newspaper article was sneaky and mean. If you wanted to talk to me, why didn't you just pick up the phone and call?"

"And you would have come running right over for a conference?"

Maggie looked down at the elevator floor as she pondered that question. Of course not, she admitted to herself. She would not have come for an interview at Adam's request. Her silence answered for her. The elevator door slid open and shut again.

"I thought not." Adam loosened his hold on her legs and let her slide down his body as he lowered her to a standing position. Every inch of her felt the electric shock. Every muscle, every plane, every ridge of his body was defined as she slid against him. The depth of feeling aroused in her by the close contact shook her, and she tried to back away from him when her feet touched the floor.

Adam hauled her roughly back into the circle of his arms. His lips took hers swiftly, unthinkingly. The kiss was hard and intense, a clashing of two stubborn wills. Standing in the elevator with the current flowing strongly between them, Adam assaulted Maggie's stubborn lips.

Her struggle to resist was brief, and unsuccessful. His lips demanded to possess her, and even as her mind recoiled in alarm, her lips flowered open beneath his. Fire licked along her nerve endings as his tongue plunged inside her mouth and began a timeless erotic rhythm. Maggie met the thrusts of his tongue with mounting passion. She wove her arms around his neck, curled her fingers in his hair, and pulled his head closer to hers.

Adam's hands explored the satiny flesh beneath her sweater, skimming around the small circle of her waist and moving up her back to press warmly into the hollow between her shoulders. Maggie leaned into him, reveling in the mutual passion of their kiss. She had the uneasy feeling that somehow she had crossed the Rubicon.

The elevator door swished open once again, and Adam lifted his head. His eyes were the turbulent blue of a storm-washed ocean. Without a word he smoothed down Maggie's sweater, took her by the hand, and practically dragged her from the elevator and down the length of the mezzanine to his office.

He pushed open the door and led her into a warm room paneled in dark mahogany, with deep brown leather chairs and a plush, cream-colored carpet. A massive desk sat in front of wide double windows that looked across the street to Calvary Baptist Church. A giant fern in a brass urn dominated one corner, and one entire wall was lined with bookshelves, floor to ceiling.

Maggie pulled herself free of Adam's hand and walked toward the bookshelves. She hadn't been prepared for what had happened to her in the elevator. She needed time to think. Running her hands lightly over the book jackets, she scanned the titles. Banking, management techniques, loans and trusts—all were titles she expected to see. Her hand stopped on a slim, leather-bound volume. *Of Mice and Men*, by Steinbeck. She pulled the volume from the shelf and flipped through the pages. Steinbeck was one of her favorite authors. How strange that Adam should have this book on his shelf, she mused.

She looked covertly at him. He was standing by the window watching her. There was a look almost of perplexity on his face, and he stood with the poised stillness of a jungle cat crouched to spring. She shoved the Steinbeck back on the shelf. The book was probably there for looks, anyhow.

"Steinbeck is a favorite author of mine." Adam

spoke quietly from his spot beside the window. "As a matter of fact, I've always wanted to play George."

Maggie looked at him, amazed. "Do you act?"

"No, I've never had the time. I thought about trying out for one of the plays when Tupelo first organized its little theater group, but there was always business to be handled."

"I can't imagine you in the role of George. I think Rhett Butler would be more your style."

" 'Frankly, mah deah, Ah don't give a damn,' " he declaimed, deadpan. Maggie laughed with him. "George appeals to me because of his compassion."

"You! Compassionate! Tell me another joke, Adam."

"If you aren't careful, Maggie, you'll discover that I'm human." Grinning broadly, Adam moved away from the window and walked to his desk. He picked up a picture and handed it to Maggie. "Beauregard, my pet. Beau for short."

Maggie took the picture with the tips of her fingers, as if it might bite. "A cat!" A fat calico cat was stretched out on a sunny window-seat, and beside him sat a slim, gray-haired woman and a handsome man, an older version of Adam. "And these must be your parents."

"Meet my family, Maggie."

She didn't want to meet his family; she wanted to grab her horn and beat a hasty retreat. It was bad enough that she had practically succumbed to him in the elevator. Finding out that he liked Steinbeck and loved his cat and had lovely parents was just too much. Adam was the enemy, she reminded herself; he was supposed to be evil right down to the bottom of his black heart.

With a sigh of regret, Maggie replaced the picture on Adam's desk. She sensed another victory for her opponent. Turning around, she saw her silver trumpet gleaming against the dark leather cushions of one of Adam's chairs. The battle wasn't over yet, she thought. "Don't try to sidetrack me."

"Nobody's trying to sidetrack you." Adam was clearly irritated with her. "Dammit, Maggie. You are the most exasperating woman I've ever met."

Good. She had made him mad. She could handle that. "And you are the most devious man *I've* ever met. Giving sneaky interviews to the press instead of facing me like a man!"

"Where's your coat, Maggie?" Adam stepped to the closet and took down his hat and topcoat.

"Why?" Maggie looked at him suspiciously. What was he up to now? she wondered. "I came here in such a hurry, I forgot my coat."

"I should have known." He clamped his hat on his head and crossed to Maggie. "Come on. We'll finish this conversation over dinner."

Maggie put her hands on her hips and faced him defiantly. "I will not have dinner with an animal assassin."

"Are you coming under your own steam, or do you want me to carry you?"

"You wouldn't!"

"Oh, no? Try me, Tigress." He took a step toward her. There was steel in his voice and icy determination in his eyes.

Maggie believed him. And she didn't relish the idea of being carried, caveman style, into a restaurant. "Okay." She glared at him. "I'll go with you. But don't assume that this is a capitulation on my part." She skirted around him as she marched out the door, head held high.

"I would never assume anything with you."

They walked in silence to Adam's car. Dusk had settled over Tupelo, and Christmas lights had been turned on all over the city. Miniature garlands and trees festooned the street lights along Main Street. Shoppers, taking advantage of late holiday shopping hours, thronged the malls.

62 • PEGGY WEBB

Maggie hugged the door handle on her side of the car and wondered if she had taken leave of her senses. She should be in her pickup truck headed home to Belden, she thought, instead of locked in a car with a devastating man who could turn her to putty with just one searing look.

After a short drive Adam parked the car behind a charming turn-of-the-century house that had been painted gray and converted into a restaurant. "Is Jefferson Place all right with you?"

"Umph," she grunted. He need not know that she would walk over coals for their fried zucchini.

Adam took her elbow to guide her up the steep steps, and she almost lost the tenuous grasp she had on her self-control. Every time he touched her, she wanted to swoon in his arms. As she seated herself in a bentwood chair beside a stained-glass window, she came to the decision that fainting benches and swooning ought to be revived. They must have been extremely convenient, she mused.

Maggie and Adam placed their orders, and he suggested that they start with fried zucchini. "I could eat my weight in the stuff," he confessed as he plunged a slice of zucchini into the bowl of dip.

It just wasn't fair that he liked fried zucchini too, Maggie thought. Morosely she dipped her vegetable, being careful to avoid colliding with Adam's hand. Sharing a bowl of dip with this man was far too intimate. Probably even sitting across the room from him would be too intimate. He had that kind of magnetism.

By the time the salads arrived, Maggie had decided that if she didn't do something fast, she would be lost forever to Adam Trent's charm, a deserter to her cause.

"I hope you understand, Adam, that I have not changed my mind about you, in spite of the fried zucchini and the calico cat."

He grinned. "You forgot Steinbeck."

"I'm serious, Adam. I still think hunters are indiscriminate killers, and nothing can change the fact that you are a hunter."

"Maggie, it's true that some hunters ignore the laws and kill indiscriminately. That doesn't mean that all hunters are monsters." Adam leaned forward to make his case. "You should know that. Aren't there more than a few bad teachers, and wouldn't you hate to be accused of inadequate teaching because of some of your colleagues?"

"How dare you compare a noble profession like teaching to the horrible practice of slaughtering wild animals!"

"That's not what I'm doing, and you know it." Adam viciously speared a piece of steak. "I'm talking about the dangers of making generalizations."

"And I'm talking about life, the life of a wild and free creature being snuffed out by a twenty-gauge shotgun just for recreation." The flames of justice were burning brightly again in Maggie's heart, and everything else was shoved down into second place.

"You're too damned stubborn to be reasonable." Adam dropped his silver onto his plate and pushed it aside. "I thought we would discuss this issue over a civilized meal, like two sane adults. I had even intended to invite you to the Waterfowls, Incorporated banquet Friday night so that you could see firsthand that some hunters are interested in preserving wildlife." He hastily scrawled his name on the check.

Maggie shoved her chair aside and stood up. "To educate me?" she asked scathingly. Her skirts swished angrily around her legs as she marched, stiff-backed, out of the restaurant.

They rode in silence back to Mutual Bank and Maggie's pickup truck. Adam parked his car in the empty space behind her truck and made a move to get out and open her car door.

"You needn't bother," she said huffily.

"Oh, but I insist," he answered, his voice dangerously quiet. She listened to the sound of his footsteps against the concrete as he stomped around to open her door. Suddenly it was jerked open, and Adam reached inside to take Maggie's hand.

Unceremoniously he pulled her from the car. The fierce night wind caught her hair and brushed it across her cheeks.

Adam stood very still, eyeing her with cold fury. And then something happened in his eyes. Maggie could see them change from ice blue to turbulent blue-gray. She lifted her chin defiantly, trembling inside at what she saw. It was naked, raw passion, and it ripped her right down the middle. Maggie Merriweather stood on Main Street with half of her heart ranting and raving for her cause and half of her straining to respond to the magnificent passion of Adam Trent.

His face softened, and his hand reached out gently to smooth back her hair. "My Lord, Maggie." He moved, and then she was in his arms. His lips claimed hers, devoured hers, as his hands reached beneath her sweater. Reason went spinning away as his tongue sought the warm inside of her mouth and his fingers grazed across the lacy top of her bra, caressing the soft skin underneath.

For a small eternity the world stood at bay while they kissed. They were no longer hunter and preservationist, but simply man and woman, locked together by the timeless bonds of desire.

It was Adam who broke the kiss, for Maggie did not have the strength. She would have stayed in his arms there in the middle of Main Street until Judgment Day.

Adam watched as Maggie gathered her splintered self together. She straightened her sweater, patted her hair, and smoothed down her skirt. There was nothing she could do to tidy up her jumbled emotions. "Thank you for the dinner," she said between stiff lips. Saying a small prayer of thanks for the manners that had provided a gracious escape, she hurried toward her truck.

She already had the door open when Adam spoke from behind her. "You forgot your horn."

"Damn," she said softly.

Five

"Maggie! That makes the third time you've called B 5," Emma Vinson chided Maggie. "Where is your mind?"

Maggie rolled her eyes heavenward. "Sorry. G 15." *My mind is still on last night,* she thought, *and it's a miracle that I lived through it.* She selected another number. Aloud, she said, "I 17." She was still amazed at herself for being in one piece. Walking back to get her trumpet from Adam after walking away from that kiss had been torture. She had felt like one of the early Christians facing the lions. "G 15," she said to her Wednesday-afternoon bingo partners at the Deerfield Nursing Home.

"You said that just a minute ago, Maggie," Fannie Mae Clark reminded her.

"Looks like we should have stolen the van and gone hunting," Emma said, chuckling. "Why didn't we, Maggie?"

"Mac is using the van to pick up supplies."

"Oh, pshaw." Fannie Mae sniffed loudly. "He could have done that tomorrow. Why didn't you tell him, Maggie? I think he's still in love with you." Fannie Mae was a subscriber to the adage, "Love conquers all."

"Phooey, Fannie Mae, Mac's not enough man for our Maggie. He doesn't hold a candle to that Adam Trent." Emma Vinson was only one of a large group of Deerfield residents who watched over Maggie's affairs with fierce maternal pride.

"Shall we continue the game, ladies?" Maggie suggested. Why couldn't Mac have been like Adam, except for the hunting? she mused. Then he would have been so easy to love, and life would have been so simple—except, maybe Adam's hunter's instinct was part of what made him exciting, and where did all that leave Maggie Merriweather? She sighed. "B 5."

Before her bingo partners could protest that B 5 had now been called four times, a very large Santa entered the game room. "Ho, ho, ho," he roared merrily. He wore the familiar red costume stuffed with pillows, and his face was completely hidden behind a luxuriant white beard and wire-rimmed glasses.

Bingo cards went flying into the air as the ladies of Deerfield surrounded Santa. Maggie wondered where in the world Mac had found such a tall Santa, and why he hadn't told her Santa was coming. She collected the cards and bingo chips as the visitor occupied her ladies. It was a game that should have been forgotten anyhow, she thought ruefully.

Out of the corner of her eye, she watched the surprise Santa chatting with her friends. He was really very good, she noted. There was a gracious ease in his manner, and he seemed to have a natural rapport with the elderly residents. She would have to congratulate Mac on his selection.

Maggie bent down to pick up a chip that had fallen to the floor. Behind her, Santa's deep voice boomed out in laughter. Maggie froze. Good land! It was Adam Trent! The voice sent shivers down her spine. She sneaked a peek over her shoulder. Santa was bent over his pack, pulling out gift-wrapped packages. He was totally immersed in his job, and paying no attention whatsoever to Maggie. She turned back around, picked up the chip, and stood up. She must have Adam Trent on the brain, she decided, and it would behoove her to forget him.

Her heels clicking smartly on the polished wooden floor as if she could drown out thoughts of Adam with their sharp, staccato rhythm, Maggie stepped across the room to the game chest. Bending over at the waist, she reached down to replace the bingo cards in the bottom drawer of the chest.

"Now, there's a view that would thaw out the North Pole." There was no mistaking Adam Trent now.

Suddenly conscious of the way her red wool jersey jump suit must be stretched across her bottom, Maggie straightened up and whirled around. "Are you sneaking around in a Santa suit just to spy on me?"

Adam laughed. "Now, Maggie. Is that any way to talk to Santa Claus?" The wire-rimmed glasses had slid down on Adam's nose, and his incredible blue eyes twinkled at her.

Maggie felt ridiculous. Of course Adam Trent wasn't sneaking around to spy on her. For one thing, he didn't sneak; he barged, and marched, and commanded.

"Truce, Maggie?"

Maggie held her hands, palms up, toward Adam in a sign of surrender. "Truce."

Adam took both her hands in his and lifted them

to his lips. He planted a kiss inside each palm, a warm, gentle kiss that made her tingle all the way down to her toes. "That's more like it, Maggie. Santa promises to be very good to you. Very good indeed," he said softly.

Maggie reclaimed her hands and tucked a stray curl behind her ear. Adam made "very good" sound like a romantic idyll between perfumed satin sheets. Or was it just her own wishful thinking? she wondered. She shook off the satin sheets and came blushingly back to Deerfield. "You make a great Santa, Adam. Do you do this often?"

"Never." His eyes raked her up and down, promising satin sheets, soft music, romantic idylls, and more. "I have ulterior motives."

Maggie laughed shakily. "They must be powerful motives." She waved her hand at his elaborate costume. "You certainly went to a lot of trouble."

"You're worth it, Maggie." They were still standing together in the corner of the large game room. Behind them the nursing-home residents were chattering gaily as they compared presents. Adam's broad back hid Maggie from view.

Maggie mentally slid between the satin sheets again, taking Adam and ecstasy with her. When she could speak, her voice was muffled. "I don't understand."

The red cap and fuzzy beard were a blur as Adam bent swiftly to claim Maggie's lips. The soft beard brushed across her face, and the pompom on the end of the cap tickled her nose. His mouth seized hers boldly, tasting, probing, exciting her. The tickling beard and the annoying pompom faded into nothingness as Maggie pressed herself against Adam.

His hands defined her body through the soft jersey of her jump suit, wrapping her waist and sliding downward over her hips. Maggie's whole body shuddered with longing for this forbidden man.

70 • PEGGY WEBB

He released her with a suddenness that startled her. "Damn," he growled. "Neither do I."

Maggie spun around and jerked the top drawer of the game chest open. Her hand moved frantically about, searching for the Christmas sheet music. "I think it would be a good idea for you to leave, Santa," she said cuttingly. How dare he kiss her like that in a public place and then back off, claiming not to understand? she raged inwardly. He was the one who had come here. "We have songs to sing." That statement didn't make sense, even to her; but she didn't care. Being around Adam Trent was getting to be more than her nerves could take. She turned around, holding the music in front of her chest like a shield. "You're blocking my way, Santa."

"Now, wait a minute, Maggie." Adam reached around her, putting his hands on the game chest, pinning her in on either side. "I didn't come here to make you mad."

"Then why did you come here? To make a spectacle of me in public?" She pressed the sheet music against his chest, trying to shove him aside.

Amusement turned up the corners of Adam's mouth. "Why, Ms. Merriweather," he drawled, "you're so good at creating your own spectacles that you certainly don't need my help." He winked broadly at her. "What's the matter, Maggie? Can't you take the heat without your horn? Or would you prefer a tabletop? Perhaps we can recreate our scene over there on top of the piano."

"I'm not interested in recreating anything with you. Now, move!"

"I haven't answered your question yet."

"I'm no longer interested in the answer."

"You're a magnificent little spitfire, and that red outfit you're wearing suits you to a tee."

"Did you mention tea, Santa?" Emma Vinson spoke up behind them. "Come on over here. We were going to serve punch and cookies a little later, but we've decided to do it right this minute." She put her tiny, blue-veined hands on Adam's sleeve and tugged. Adam turned to face her, and she clucked her tongue. "There you are, Maggie. I thought you had gone out to steal a van for us."

"Emma . . ." Maggie began warningly.

"Maggie steals vans?" Santa raised his bushy white brows at Maggie and chuckled. "I might have known."

"Of course," Emma said serenely. "Our Maggie will do anything for us." Emma Vinson stopped dead in her tracks, her lace-up, rubber-soled shoes squeaking on the wooden floor. "How do you know our Maggie?" She peered keenly up at him, her brown eyes snapping. "Do I know you?"

"Emma, Santa Claus is Adam Trent." Maggie hoped that Emma would remember the significance of the name before she prattled on and revealed their reason for being in the Holly Springs National Forest the Wednesday before.

Emma peered around Adam's broad chest at Maggie. "*The* Adam Trent?" she inquired breathlessly.

Maggie nodded her head.

"Oh, my," Emma breathed. She remembered. She also remembered the way he had held Maggie's hands at the gas station. And she loved romance far more than she did intrigue. She grabbed Maggie's hand and thrust it toward Adam. He took it automatically. "Maggie, you bring Santa on over to the punch table. I think he's earned a little something to drink. I've got to go tell Fannie Mae." Emma scooted off with a spryness that belied her seventy-six years.

Adam chuckled. "I like that lady." He held Maggie's hand as if he had not the slightest intention of ever letting go.

"Mrs. Emma Vinson. She was already a resident

when I started coming here, three years ago. She's a remarkable lady. Mac says she fought and overcame cancer about five years ago."

"Mac? The one who is still in love with you?" Adam stopped and looked down into her face. There was something in his eyes that she couldn't quite fathom.

"Who told you that?"

"I overheard it when I came in."

"You were eavesdropping?"

"No. I was standing in the doorway, adjusting my pack. I heard somebody say Mac is still in love with you."

Maggie laughed. "If you believe everything these dear ladies say about me, you'll think I'm the most sought-after woman in Lee County. They're prejudiced, and they fantasize a lot."

"Who is Mac?" Adam Trent was pursuing the subject with a single-mindedness that amazed Maggie. What possible difference could it make to Adam? she wondered.

"Mac Jennings is director of Deerfield and a friend of mine. A long time ago we were engaged."

"And he let you go?" Was that amusement or amazement in Adam's face? It was hard for her to tell behind all the whiskers.

"As a matter of fact, he insisted that I go." Maggie chuckled, remembering Mac's perspiring, flustered face when he broke their engagement. "Mac couldn't understand my ardor for causes. Few people do."

They were standing now at the punch table. The ladies of Deerfield had outdone themselves with the decorations. A white felt cloth appliquéd with Christmas trees, snowmen, and Santas covered the rectangular table. Three wise men, made with leftover scraps of satin and lace and decorated with discarded rhinestone jewelry, sat among the holly and mistletoe in the center of the table. A mouth-watering assortment of cookies was stacked high on the trays surrounding the punch bowl.

Adam attacked the cookies with the eagerness of a two-year-old. "Maggie," he said, grinning up from his laden plate, "how about joining the Adam Trent cause?"

"What cause is that?"

"Rescuing a poor, deprived banker from starvation."

"From the looks of your plate, I'd say you don't need any help. Haven't you eaten today, Adam?"

"Not since breakfast. The Board meeting was a bear, and then there was a minor crisis in the loan department . . ." He let the sentence trail off as he looked from Maggie to his plate. "If you'll sit with me on that sofa over there, I'll tell you why I came to Deerfield today." He smiled that brilliant smile, the one she knew would melt all the dummies at Madame Tussaud's into puddles, and Maggie capitulated.

She didn't capitulate, really, she told herself as she followed Adam to the brown tweed sofa. There was no good reason not to join him. She was, after all, twenty-eight years old and perfectly capable of carrying on a normal conversation with a normal man. She glanced covertly at his profile as he sat beside her devouring cookies. Perfectly fabulous man would be more like it, she thought, even in that Santa suit.

She was strongly attracted to him, and she knew it. Would she be forced to make a terrible choice between Adam and the cause she believed in so fervently?

"Have a chocolate-chip cookie, Maggie." Adam leaned over and stuffed one into her mouth. He laughed as a few crumbs fell on her chin, and he reached up to wipe them away. "I'm afraid I took more than I can eat."

The ordinary gesture made her shiver with

delight. She straightened her back and inched away from Adam on the sofa. There was no choice, she decided. She wouldn't allow their involvement to go that far. Could a few impulsive kisses be called an involvement? That was stretching credibility when the other person was Tupelo's most eligible bachelor. She relaxed at the thought.

"I'm waiting, Adam."

"For another cookie?"

She grimaced at him. "For an explanation. Did anybody ever tell you that you are the world's most maddening man?"

"Only my calico cat."

"Adam," Maggie said threateningly.

He winked. "Sorry about that." Placing the empty plate on the coffee table in front of them, Adam turned a serious face back to Maggie. "I came to Deerfield today to invite you to attend the Waterfowls, Incorporated banquet with me Friday night." He held up his hands to quiet her protest. "Before you say no, hear me out. I believe you will learn some things at WI that will help you to understand my viewpoint, the hunter's viewpoint."

"I understand all I want to about the hunter's viewpoint. I don't need *educating* by you." The word dripped with contempt in remembrance of the challenge he had flung at her that day in the woods of Boguefala Bottom.

"Dammit, Maggie. I came here to make peace with you, not to start another fight."

"Who's starting another fight?" She batted her lashes innocently at him. "I just turned you down, and you got testy."

Adam sat very still on his end of the sofa. It was a controlled, icy stillness. "What are you afraid of, Maggie?"

What if she told him the truth? she thought. What if she said, "Adam, I'm afraid my attraction for you will make me lose sight of my goal"? He'd probably laugh all the way back to that stuffy bank of his. He had made his feelings for her exceedingly plain: She was a challenge for him, and he intended to "tame" her. Well, not while she still had possession of her senses, thank you very much.

She lifted her chin so that she could give him one of her haughty looks. At least, that was what her brother, Jim, called it. "Don't flatter yourself, Adam. I'm not afraid of anything, particularly you."

Adam's muscles strained forward, almost as if he were reaching out to touch her, but he never left his seat. "Stubborn Maggie," he whispered. "Of course you're not afraid of me. Any fool can see that."

The moment stretched between them, heavy with unspoken emotion. At last Adam stood up. "Call me if you change your mind."

He left her sitting on the sofa and walked toward the center of the room to say good-bye to the Deerfield residents. Emma and Fannie Mae patted his arm and cooed over him. And he loved every minute of it, Maggie noted angrily. Her hands curled into tight fists as she watched him. Dammit! Why did he have to do everything so well? He could at least be a hater of little old ladies. Then she could happily mow him down and leave him bleeding on the pavement without a backward glance.

Maggie's teeth worried her lower lip as she watched Adam Trent, alias Santa, make his way to the door. She almost ran after him to say that she had changed her mind about the banquet, but instead she picked up his empty plate and carried it to the kitchen. Maggie had never before backed away from a real challenge. Her retreat from Adam was uncharacteristic. She slammed the plate into the sink with unnecessary vigor. Broken glass tinkled against the porcelain sink as the plate shattered. It was all Adam's fault, Maggie fumed, muttering as she picked up the pieces. There wouldn't be an unbroken piece of china left in Tupelo if she continued to react like this to these unsettling encounters with him.

She finished picking up the party plates (with no more "accidents"), apologized to her ladies for leaving Deerfield so early, and headed home to Belden. She needed to talk to somebody.

As soon as she had parked her pickup, she went around the side of her cottage and across her backyard toward Martha Jo's house. Sam picked up a stick between his teeth and trotted after her, wagging his tail. He was hopefully eager for a game of fetch.

Maggie bent down and patted his head. "Not today, boy." His eyes looked up at her so mournfully that she relented and tossed the stick. "Just once," she told him.

Leaving Sam bounding after his stick, Maggie entered the small thicket of pine trees that divided her property from Martha Jo's. The quiet solitude of the trees soothed her as she passed through them on the way to the small redwood cottage on the edge of the woods.

Martha Jo had seen her coming and stood holding the door open. The light from inside the cottage made a bright path on the brittle grass under Maggie's feet. "It must be important or you wouldn't have come after a long day at school and an afternoon of bingo." Martha Jo always got right to the heart of the matter. That was one of the reasons she was Maggie's best friend.

"I need your advice," Maggie told her as she stepped into the warm cottage. Walking into Martha Jo's house was like stepping into a museum. Antique tables, railroad lanterns, brass spittoons, and even an old buggy seat decorated the den.

Martha Jo swept a stack of student papers aside

and motioned for Maggie to sit on the sofa. "Fire away."

"It's Adam Trent."

"I thought so." She waited for Maggie to continue.

Maggie smiled fondly at her friend. Martha Jo's hair looked like a rag mop, and she generally supplied a stream of witty banter that kept people laughing; but when the chips were down, she could be counted on for good, solid advice. "Adam and I are avowed enemies over this hunting business, but every time we are together, the sparks fly." She hesitated and then plunged ahead. "Somehow, we always end up in each other's arms."

"What's wrong with that, Maggie? He's a powerfully attractive man."

"In more ways than you know," Maggie murmured. She jumped up from the sofa and began to pace the floor. "It's just that . . . dammit! He's a hunter."

"And that makes him one hundred percent evil?" Martha Jo raised skeptical eyebrows. "Come on, Maggie. You know there's no dividing line between good and evil."

Maggie leaned her elbow on the oak mantel and looked down into the fire. "He's asked me to go to the Waterfowls, Incorporated banquet with him Friday night."

"Do you want to go?"

"Yes . . . and no. I'm torn right down the middle by this whole thing. If Adam were different and if I were different, there wouldn't be a problem. As it is, I feel like going to the banquet with him would be compromising my principles."

"And that's what life is all about, isn't it, Maggie? Compromise."

Maggie whirled around from the fire and smiled

at her friend. "Compromise is not capitulation, is it?"

"Nobody ever said it was."

"Lead me to the phone."

"Now you're talking." Martha Jo uncrossed her legs and jumped up from the sofa. "I think I'll have a cup of coffee, Maggie. Do you want one?"

Maggie looked up from the phone book, holding her finger in the T's so she wouldn't lose her place. "Ugh!"

Six

Maggie's ponytail cascaded down the back of her shocking red football jersey, Number 90, a souvenir of her college dating days. She hitched up her army pants and tackled the mass of second-grade papers spread over her kitchen table.

In the middle of her second set of two plus two's, the doorbell rang. She wasn't expecting anybody, but company was always a welcome diversion.

Adam Trent stood in her doorway, immaculate and handsome in a dark gray business suit.

Maggie clutched her door handle until her knuckles turned white. "Today is Thursday."

"I know." He smiled. "May I come in?" And then he was inside her den. Without waiting for a "Yes, of course" or a "Please do," he just marched right in and made himself at home.

"I thought the banquet was tomorrow night." She put the antique rocking chair between her and her unexpected guest. Oh, damn! she agonized. Why had she made that phone call and why was he so scrumptious and why was he *here?* She felt suddenly as shy and tongue-tied as some of her own students.

"It is." He smiled that enchanting, disarming smile, the one that made her forget his hunting and his biased opinions of FOA and his high-handed way of kissing her. "I'm on my way to the library to hear a lecture on socioeconomic trends in the Soviet Union, and I thought you might like to join me."

Was he kidding? she wondered. Socioeconomic trends in the Soviet Union? She'd just as soon sit through a tooth-pulling exhibition.

"I know I should have called to see if you already had plans, but I came on . . . impulse." The slight hesitation indicated just how foreign "impulse" was to Adam Trent's nature. He had never done anything on impulse until he met Maggie, and she sensed it.

"I'm swamped with papers to grade, and, to be quite frank with you, I'm not in the right frame of mind for a lecture that highbrow."

Adam peeled off his jacket and draped it casually across the back of her sofa. Loosening his tie, he grinned at Maggie. "To tell you the truth, I'm not either. Where are those papers?"

Maggie watched him in amazement. Just what did he think he was doing? "You're not suggesting what I think you are, are you?"

"Yes. I'm quite good at second-grade math. A whiz, in fact." He rolled up his sleeves. "You did say you were 'swamped'?" His left eyebrow inclined over his dazzling blue eyes. "I'm offering my assistance."

Maggie clutched the back of her rocking chair and tried to breathe normally. How could she trust a man who paraded around in a Santa Claus suit? He had to be up to something. "I don't think that's a good idea."

"Why not?"

"Well, because . . ." Because he looked good enough to eat and because he wore three-piece suits and she wore football jerseys and because she just wouldn't be responsible for her actions if he stayed in her cozy little house a minute longer. ". . . because I draw smiley faces on the papers."

"You do what?"

"You know. Smiley faces. Circles with a grinning mouth. It adds a personal touch and makes the kids feel good about their work."

"It doesn't sound too hard to me. "Now"—he rubbed his palms together—"where are those papers?"

"If you hurry, you can probably still get a good seat at the lecture."

Adam threw back his head and laughed. "You're about as subtle as a bulldozer." He crossed over to the rocking chair and covered Maggie's hands with his. "Don't deprive me of doing this good deed, helping a schoolteacher in distress." He was standing so close Maggie could see the laugh lines fanning out from his eyes. "Besides, this will give us a chance to get to know each other better."

Maggie jerked her hands away and stepped backward. "This way," she said curtly as she whirled and almost ran to her kitchen table. Anything was better than standing so close beside him she practically sizzled. She would put the kitchen table between them.

But Adam had other ideas. He dragged his chair up close to Maggie's. "I have to see how you draw these smiley faces," he explained.

Maggie was intoxicated by his nearness. The faint, woodsy scent of his after-shave reminded her of the times she had encountered him in the forest, of their heated arguments, of their vows to fight each other, but most of all, of their kisses. Getting to know Adam Trent would be walking right into danger. And Maggie loved danger.

Taking a deep breath, she cocked her head, smiled at him, and jumped in with both feet. "I'll expect no mistakes from you, Mr. Trent," she said saucily as she handed him a stack of math papers. "My students are accustomed to perfection."

"Dear me, Miss Merriweather, I was always taught that humbleness is a virtue."

"You have been hoodwinked, Mr. Trent. Self-confidence is my motto."

He grinned, thoroughly enjoying their banter. "Some would say arrogance."

"Only the uneducated, the uninformed, the untidy, and the undeserving."

"You left out one."

"What?"

"The ugly."

"Well, of course! Thank you, Mr. Trent."

"Fortunately, I don't fall into any of those categories. I am a humble admirer of your 'self-confidence.' "

"If you hadn't said that, I was going to black your eyes."

"How would I ever explain that at my board meetings?" And that was the last time board meetings were mentioned, for Maggie and Adam were both enchanted with the easy camaraderie that existed between them. They became completely caught up in a lighthearted mood that took them far away from board meetings and seminars and three-piece suits and impulsive doings with trumpets and belly-dancing costumes.

The jumbled mass of papers rapidly became neat stacks of corrected work.

"How about a tea break?" Maggie suggested.

"Make that hot chocolate and show me where the fixings are," Adam said.

While Adam made the chocolate, Maggie walked

into the den to put a record on the stereo. "What kind of music do you like?" she called to him.

"Almost anything except hard rock."

Maggie selected an album of haunting blues, the kind of music that grabbed the heart and turned it inside out. She turned the volume up so that they could hear it in the kitchen and then joined Adam.

"How is that?"

"Perfect. I love blues, especially the Bourbon Street variety played by that tremendous clarinetist." He handed her a cup of hot chocolate.

His fingers lingered on hers as the cup exchanged hands, and their eyes met and held for a searing instant. Maggie's lips parted and she held her breath, waiting for the moment to pass. Here was more danger than she had bargained for. A man who made her weak-kneed and who loved her kind of music. Not only that, but he could even identify the instrument being played. Adam Trent was full of surprises.

"Adam." It was a shattered plea, a useless denial of the current that flowed between them.

His lips found hers over the chocolate cup, and there could be no more denial. The lightest caress, like the kiss of the morning sun against dewdrops, touched her parted lips, and Maggie was caught up once again in the magic that was Adam Trent.

It was a gentle tasting as Maggie precariously balanced the cup between them, a soft touching of flesh that quickly fanned the flames of passion between them and demanded more.

Adam's hands cupped her face as the kiss deepened, and Maggie nearly tipped the cup of chocolate onto him. She kissed him with a wild abandon, letting go of all her reservations. She was controlled by her obsession for this man, and nothing mattered except the moment.

Adam groaned deep in his throat, and his hands roamed under her football jersey. Her soft flesh flamed at his touch, and she arched against him, begging for more. The forgotten chocolate cascaded from the overturned cup, running down the back of Adam's neck and soaking through his white shirt.

His startled protest was muffled against her mouth, as slowly they came out of the spell that bound them.

"Your shirt!" Maggie cried. "Oh, I'm sorry!"

He lifted the wet material away from his neck and grinned. "I've always thought chocolate becomes me."

Maggie laughed with him, and the minor accident became the perfect means for breaking the tension between them. Fortunately, the chocolate had cooled during their kiss, so there was no real damage done except for the mess on Adam's shirt and Maggie's kitchen floor.

They argued good-naturedly over who should have custody of the mop, and Adam won. Maggie abandoned her shoes and swabbed at the puddles of chocolate with wads of paper towels. She ended up getting more chocolate on her feet than on the towels.

"I think you've discovered a new nail polish," Adam said, teasing.

"Yes, but would it sell?"

"Maybe to a few hungry cats." Adam laid the mop aside and stripped off his wet shirt.

Maggie stifled a gasp. What was he doing? Oh, that chest! That magnificent bare chest! Her eyes seemed glued to the spot. She thought she was going to have heart failure right there in the middle of her kitchen floor, chocolate toes and all. *Oh, Lord,* she prayed, *don't let me attack this man with my mop and drag him off to the bedroom caveman style.*

"I thought I would toss this shirt into your washing machine." He stood with the wet shirt dangling from one hand.

Once in the bedroom, her fantasy continued, she would proceed to gobble him up, piece by piece, lingering longest over the chocolate parts, until there was no more Adam; and she, Maggie the cat, would be sitting in bed, purring.

"You do have a washing machine, don't you?"

She might save a little piece for tomorrow, she decided, for she would definitely be sorry when there was no more Adam.

"Maggie?"

"What?" The real man with the—oh, no, she couldn't even look at that chest without panting—soggy shirt was speaking to her. "Yes, the machine. In there." She pointed to her utility room. "Don't trip on the—"

"Damn!"

". . . garden rake." She peered around the door. "Are you all right in there?"

"A sizable lump on my head notwithstanding, I'm just dandy." He dropped the shirt into the machine, added powder, and closed the lid. "What is a garden rake doing in here? It's the dead of winter."

"Sometimes it comes in handy for my carpet."

"You rake your carpet?" He started the machine.

"No. When I lose things in my carpet, I find them with the garden rake."

"How innovative." He emerged from the utility room, and she had to calm her galloping heart and still her runaway thoughts once more. It wasn't fair that he looked twice as good without his shirt as she had imagined.

She was staring, and he knew it. The slow grin started at his mouth and moved upward to his eyes. "Is something wrong?"

Covering her flaming face, she croaked, "I'll get you a shirt."

"I don't think it will fit." His smile was now positively gloating.

"It's Jim's," she said as she whirled around and retreated from the room. Oh, damn! she muttered to herself. He was *supposed* to be the enemy. In the guest room, she banged open several dresser drawers before she found a couple of shirts that Jim always kept at her house. Her brother was fond of popping in for visits that turned into all-night gab sessions. Jim so enjoyed being "spontaneous" that he had suits of clothes scattered all over Lee County at the homes of his friends.

Yanking out the shirt, Maggie marched back to the kitchen, determined to clothe Adam and send him on his way. Enough was enough, she thought. She had to teach school tomorrow, and it was going to take her the rest of the night and part of tomorrow just to recover from the sight of Adam's bare chest. Why couldn't Mac's chest have looked like that?

"Here." She thrust the shirt unceremoniously at him. "Put this on."

"Yes, ma'am!" Adam gave her a teasing military salute.

"Thank you for helping me grade papers. I'll get your coat." She tried to keep a stiff upper lip, but standing there with her ponytail, and chocolate on her bare feet, she didn't look very forbidding.

"Is this the brush-off?" Adam leaned against the kitchen closet and took his time buttoning Jim's shirt. When he had finished, he flashed her a lazy smile that melted the chocolate on her toes. "I haven't had my chocolate yet."

Maggie pulled her eyes away from Adam's mesmerizing smile and looked down at her toes. She had to get him out of her house. Being here alone with him was simply too dangerous. He was so friendly and charming, not to mention perfectly devastating, that she kept forgetting who he was. "It's cold now. And besides, I'm going skating."

Adam gave his head a puzzled shake. "Did I miss something? I thought you said, 'I'm going skating.' "

"I did. I like to roller-skate." It was true. She did like to skate. "It's a good way to relax after grading papers." She'd never used it for that reason before, but it sounded plausible enough. She knew she'd say anything to get Adam Trent to leave before she lost control completely and did something really foolish. Like locking him in her bedroom and throwing away the key.

With deliberation, Adam assessed the woman standing before him. She was bold and beautiful, he thought, warm and playful as a cocker-spaniel puppy and cocky as a bantam rooster. And she was totally fascinating. "I'll go with you."

"But"—Damn, she thought. This wasn't working out right at all—"men who wear three-piece suits don't roller-skate."

"I'll change. Get me a pair of jeans." He laughed joyously at her look of frustration. "Jim's jeans. Surely he left a pair of jeans to go with this shirt."

"You're impossible!" she yelled. "You come barging into my house and commandeer my second-grade papers and . . ." It was mostly the kiss. Her face flamed at the memory of how much she had enjoyed his kiss, how much she enjoyed all his kisses. Then she barged ahead, full steam. ". . . and spill chocolate. I will not take a banker who spills chocolate, roller-skating. Besides, I'll bet you haven't been skating since you were five!"

"Guilty." He grinned, then breezed past her. "Is this the way to the spare bedroom?"

She clenched her teeth and rolled her eyes heavenward. "Now who's being a bulldozer?" She could hear him whistling as he sauntered down the hall to her spare bedroom. Abruptly the whistling ceased. Now what was he up to? she wondered. Maggie tiptoed to the kitchen door and cocked her head, listening. She didn't want Adam to know that she cared a hoot about what he was doing back there.

The closet door banged, and Adam called down the hall. "Better wash your feet and put on your shoes if you want to go skating with me."

Maggie stuck out her tongue and picked up her shoes. Well, heck, she decided, he was just as stubborn as she. In the bathroom she thought about taking the soap, marching down the hall, and conking him on his arrogant head. Then she changed her mind and decided that skating would be fun after all, especially if Adam Trent fell on his backside.

She grinned at the thought all the way to Circus Skating Center. Maggie and Adam shed their coats and checked out two pairs of roller skates. Except for a small party of giggling thirteen-year-old girls, the rink was empty.

Loud rock music blared over the speakers, and strobe lights flashed. Adam kept a firm grip on the rail as he made a wobbly entry onto the rink. "I don't remember roller-skating being like this," he shouted above the music.

"It wasn't, thirty years ago," she answered gleefully. She took a quick spin around the rink and came back to Adam. He was easing carefully around the edge of the floor, within grabbing distance of the rail.

"I don't remember the floor's being so far away," he said ruefully.

"It wasn't—"

"Don't say it," he warned her.

"Come on, Adam. Nobody forgets how to skate. Not even stuffy bankers in three-piece suits."

"Did you say stuffy? I take that as a challenge, madam." He ventured bravely toward the center of the rink. After a shaky start, his confidence on wheels returned. "I'll race you around the rink."

"Prepare to lose." Maggie did a neat pivot and spun off across the floor.

"I never lose."

Maggie looked over her shoulder at him. "Not bad for a man your age."

"Minx." His hands flailed the air as his legs threatened to go in two different directions. "Wait till I catch you," he shouted when his feet were back under control.

The clatter of their wheels was drowned out by the music, and their faces changed from purple to red to blue in the strobe lights. Maggie felt a wild exhilaration as she raced ahead of Adam. It didn't matter whether they were confronting each other in the woods, matching wits at a banking seminar, or chatting in her den. Being with Adam made every inch of her feel alive.

She glanced back over her shoulder in time to watch Adam's uncertain negotiation of a curve. He was a big man, and she knew he'd make quite a splat on the floor if he fell. He might even break something. Suddenly, Maggie didn't want to see him flat on the floor.

She whirled around and raced toward him.

"Maag-gie!"

She reached out her hand, but Adam was already on the way down. He grabbed for her, and the two of them fell in a tangled heap onto the wooden floor. His breath whooshed out as Maggie landed on top of him.

"Are you all right?" She looked anxiously into his face. He'd gotten the brunt of it by breaking her fall, and, besides, she was accustomed to an occasional spill on the rink.

"I think I'm dying," he said over a groan.

Maggie grabbed his head with both hands. "Oh, Lord, Adam. Do you need a doctor?" Sheer panic seized her. Not Adam. Adam couldn't be hurt. What if he were seriously injured? She just couldn't bear it. "Say something, Adam."

"I think you'd better help me. Quick."

Her nose was now almost touching his as she scanned his face for signs of trouble. His blue eyes twinkled up at her. Somehow, she thought, he didn't look like a suffering man.

"I have one last request, Maggie. Kiss me before I die." He couldn't suppress his grin any longer.

"I ought to kill you." She pulled away from him and tried to glare, but she was too relieved to look very formidable.

Adam cupped her cheeks with his hands and kissed the tip of her nose. "I always grab opportunity."

"The name is Maggie." She was acutely conscious of the long, lean body underneath her. And, although the skating rink was dark except for the occasional illumination of the flashing strobe lights, she didn't think Tupelo was ready for what she was thinking. "Or have you forgotten?" she finished breathlessly.

"No, indeed. I haven't forgotten." His lips seared briefly across hers. It was a butterfly kiss, but it felt like an inferno to Maggie. "Upsy-daisy." Adam sat up and dumped her onto the floor beside him. "I won." He crossed his legs, Indian fashion, and smiled triumphantly.

"What do you mean, you won? Get up from there and I'll show you who won." She leaned over and tweaked his ear.

"Mr. *Trent?*"

Startled, Maggie and Adam looked up at the prim-faced matron towering over them. She was standing outside the rink, staring across the railing, and her disbelieving eyes swung from Adam to Maggie and back again.

For a man who had been so near death a minute

before, he moved with alacrity, Maggie thought wryly as Adam stood up. She decided to watch from the floor.

"Mrs. Vandergelding. What brings you to the rink at this time of evening?"

Smooth, that was what he was, she thought admiringly. Adam Trent managed to make Jim's plaid flannel shirt and tight jeans look like a fashion ad.

"My granddaughter and her friends are having a party. I came to pick them up." Mrs. Vandergelding's eyebrows lifted close to her henna-dyed bangs as she took in Adam's attire. "I didn't know you skated, Mr. Trent."

Maggie thought that the woman made skating sound like one of the seven deadly sins. She made a face and tapped her fingernails on the floor.

"This is the first time I've skated in—"

"Thirty years," Maggie said from the floor.

". . . a long time."

Mrs. Vandergelding looked down her nose at Maggie, and her eyebrows moved an inch higher. "You haven't introduced me to your . . ." She let the sentence trail off as if she couldn't find words to describe Maggie.

With lithe grace, Maggie unfolded her long legs and stood up. "Sweetie." She smoothed her red football jersey over her slim hips in a deliberately provocative manner and then clutched Adam's arm. "I call him my sugar daddy, and he calls me his sweetie." She smiled archly at Mrs. Vandergelding.

Mrs. Vandergelding's breath whistled through her teeth as if somebody had socked her in the stomach.

If Adam's look could have killed, Maggie knew she would be dead on the spot. "Don't mind my cousin, Mrs. Vandergelding. She likes to tease."

"Your cousin?" Mrs. Vandergelding squeaked out.

"I'm not—"

Adam gave Maggie a sharp tweak on the bottom. "She's wild about skating. Talked me into coming with her tonight. I think I see your granddaughter waiting up front. It's been so good to see you, Mrs. Vandergelding. Tell Sam 'hello' for me." He kept up a continuous stream of chatter so that Maggie couldn't drop in another bombshell.

After Mrs. Vandergelding and the girls had left the rink, Adam grabbed Maggie's hand and propelled her toward the door. His face was grim.

"Can't you take a joke? Mrs. Vander-what's-her-name looked like a snob whose balloon needed puncturing."

"And you take on all stuffed shirts and snobs, right, Maggie?" He unlaced his skates and jerked them off his feet.

"Well, you needn't be so huffy about it!" She flung her skates on the counter and grabbed her coat.

The December wind blasted them as they left the rink. "Mrs. Vandergelding may be a pain in the—"

"Adam!"

". . . but her husband is one of my most valued customers." He turned the key in the ignition and the Mercedes came to life. He swung the car onto Highway 6 and headed into Tupelo.

Maggie groaned. She'd done it again. If she lived to be a hundred, would she ever learn to look before she leaped? "I'm sorry, Adam."

"It's okay." Only the hum of the engine and the swish of tires against pavement interrupted the silence. Gradually the tension eased out of Adam's face, and he looked over at Maggie in the darkness. "It really is okay. There have been plenty of times when I've wanted to puncture Mrs. Vandergelding's balloon. And, Maggie"—he grinned—"you do it with such pizzazz."

Maggie smiled back. "Adam, can we stop at Finney's? I need to console myself with food."

"A chicken-salad sandwich would be nice," he agreed.

"I was thinking more in terms of a banana split with double fudge and gobs of whipped cream with nuts and two cherries on top."

"It figures."

Maggie watched Adam as he made his way across the crowded room toward her. She still couldn't believe she was actually here, after that blooper she had pulled at the skating rink last night, but Adam was determined that she see hunting from the hunter's point of view. Imagine! she thought, Maggie Merriweather at a duck hunters' banquet! Not that it would change her mind, of course. No matter how much she admired Adam or how much her foolish heart pounded at the sight of his handsome face—and, oh, Lord, he was devastating as he moved toward her—she would never understand the hunter's point of view.

"Somebody said you are Maggie Merriweather." A beefy-jowled man thrust his red face toward Maggie and spoke belligerently. "Women ought to stay out of a man's affairs." He glared at her and then took another big gulp of bourbon. "My wife knows her place," he said proudly.

"How often do you let her out of the cage?" Maggie asked sweetly. She really wanted to knock him back into the dark ages, where he belonged.

The man's red face got even redder. "Somebody ought to teach you a lesson," he sputtered.

Suddenly Adam appeared behind the man. With a swiftness that made Maggie's detractor spill his drink over his shirt, Adam gripped the man's arm and pulled him away from Maggie. His face was hard as a piece of flint. "George, I hope you have made my guest welcome." He pronounced "my guest" as if it were a title given by a powerful monarch.

"*You* brought her?" George turned a disbelieving face toward Adam.

"Yes. Negotiation is better than confrontation. Don't you agree?" Adam's face dared George to take issue.

George looked from the stunning activist in the white wool dress to the banker with the barely controlled anger. "I need another drink," he muttered as he slunk away.

"I apologize, Maggie," Adam told her after the man left. "I had hoped that sort of behavior wouldn't occur tonight. I want you to get a good impression of our group of duck hunters."

Maggie took the drink he held out to her. "You have nothing to apologize for, Adam," she said. Except, she added silently, for being so devastatingly wonderful, he made her cause dim around the edges. She took a deep breath to steady herself. It had been like that ever since Adam had picked her up at her cottage that evening. He made her feel as if she were on a runaway roller coaster, hurtling through space to an unknown destination.

Adam smiled. "You're a trouper, Maggie." He took her arm. "Let's find our seats. I think they're getting ready to serve the meal."

They made slow progress across the crowded room to the banquet table.

Steaming platters of boiled shrimp shipped up from the Gulf vied for space on the groaning table with deep-fried crab claws, seafood gumbo, and a dish that looked suspiciously like frog legs.

"That's not what I think it is"—Maggie nodded at

the platters of fried frog legs—"is it, Adam?" She wrinkled her nose in distaste.

"Don't tell me you are personal friends with frogs too." Adam looked at her and laughed.

"They look like they still ought to be on the creek bank belly-flopping, or whatever they do."

"How do you feel about shrimp?"

"Somehow I could never get personally involved with anything as ugly as a shrimp."

"Good. I'd hate for you to waste away to nothing just because I brought you to the WI banquet."

"Did somebody say 'waste away'? With all that food?" Maggie and Adam turned to see a handsome young couple standing behind them. "It's been a long time, Trent." The lanky, sandy-haired man stuck out his hand.

"Harold Ryan!" Adam took the man's hand in a firm grip. "And Anna!" Turning to Maggie, he made the introductions.

Anna Ryan's white teeth flashed in her pert, freckled face as she smiled at Maggie. "I've heard so much about you. I've always admired women who fight for what they believe in."

"Considering the nature of my cause, I never expected to hear that here tonight."

"I hope you'll hear other things that will surprise you." Anna smiled warmly. "We're not such a bad lot."

Maggie glanced at Adam's handsome profile and back at the Ryans. They certainly weren't, she thought. Not bad at all.

The four of them sat down at a table and were joined by Mr. and Mrs. Rayford Sanburn Smith III. While Mrs. Smith held the floor with a monologue about her latest redecorating, she studied Maggie through narrowed eyes. She had heard about the younger woman at the beauty shop.

"Tell me, dear," she said when she had finished

her recital. "Don't you have anything better to do than run around the country protesting?"

Maggie looked her squarely in the eye. "No, Mrs. Smith. I'm a garden-club reject. I have to fill my lonely hours with something."

"Bravo, Maggie," Adam whispered into her ear.

Anna Ryan tapped her fork against her water glass. "Hear, hear!" she said, and grinned at Maggie. Harold Ryan winked at her.

"Well, my Rayford wouldn't allow me to make a fool of myself like that," Mrs. Smith said with a sniff.

"It must be stultifying to require his permission for everything, Mrs. Smith." Maggie dunked her shrimp into the tartar sauce and continued matter-of-factly. "You have my sympathy." She felt only slightly wicked for having bared her claws.

Adam touched her arm in a brief gesture of reassurance and support. Maggie smiled at him. He had been right that day in his office. He was human. Knowing that deepened her dilemma. She was already teetering on the brink of a precipice where Adam was concerned. She didn't need much encouragement to tip her over the edge.

Harold Ryan came to Maggie's defense. "I admire a spunky woman. Maggie's not a monster just because she disagrees with us."

"Right," Anna added.

Mrs. Smith's face was a thundercloud, and as she opened her mouth to speak, Adam deftly stepped in and turned the conversation away from Maggie and her activities.

Maggie gazed at his strong profile, and her heart rose into her throat. Her mind only half-followed the conversation that swirled around her. Tonight's banquet was not, after all, a matter of principle; it was a matter of the heart. The seafood gumbo turned to sawdust in her mouth as the terrible choice loomed closer.

She glanced sideways at Adam. His incredible smile was turned in Anna Ryan's direction. The man had more than his share of charm, she admitted. And he probably knew it. Were all his charm and compassion just a part of his scheme to get under her skin, to "tame" her? Maggie told herself stoutly that she hoped so. Life would be so much simpler if that were true. She stiffened her spine and mentally geared herself for battle, but the gumbo still tasted like sawdust, and somewhere deep inside her a small, glowing flame refused to be extinguished.

A balding man with a paunch stood behind the podium at the head table and rapped his gavel.

"The auction is about to begin," Adam whispered as he leaned over to Maggie. He pulled his chair away from the table so that he could get a better view of the podium. The maneuver positioned his chair only inches from Maggie, so that his right thigh brushed intimately against her left leg.

Was the move calculated? she wondered. Even if not, it was so dreadfully disconcerting that Maggie had a hard time following the speaker's words.

"Before we begin the auction," the man at the podium began, "I want to thank all of you for supporting Waterfowls, Incorporated. As you know, the money we raise provides breeding grounds for many species of ducks, breeds that were being killed at an alarming rate in the early nineteen-hundreds, until we stepped in. We as hunters can be proud of our conservation efforts. Our hunting controls the duck population so that it doesn't grow too big for the breeding grounds to support it, and our money furnishes a place for them to breed safely. And now, without further ado, let's see how much money we can raise this year." He held up a large limited-edition print of a covey of quail. "What am I bid for this jewel?"

Adam spoke quietly in Maggie's ear. "Now do you believe me?"

"Who was killing all the ducks in the first place?" she hissed. She had not known that WI worked to save the duck population, but she still doubted that they did it out of any real concern for the well-being of the ducks.

The auction moved quickly as people bid for the limited-edition prints of pictures painted by some of America's leading wildlife artists. Adam paid an outrageous sum for a beautiful print of bufflehead ducks on a lake covered in morning mists. He obviously didn't have to pinch pennies the way schoolteachers did, Maggie thought. She admired the print and was totally unconscious of how Adam watched her eyes sparkle as she heaped sincere praise on the picture and the artist.

After the auction was over, Adam took Maggie's elbow and steered her through the crowd. He went the long way around the room to avoid further contact with Maggie's detractors. Or, she wondered, was it so that he could prolong the time Maggie's back was crushed against his chest as they were buffeted by the crowd? She wasn't sure, but in either case it was disconcerting.

She held her breath as they stepped out into the cold December night. Now he would let go and she could breathe again. But it was not so. Adam moved his hand down to her waist as they walked toward his car. The dim lights of the parking lot cast an eerie glow on her white dress, and Adam's hand looked darkly foreign as it rested there. Maggie wondered if he could hear her heart pounding, and then swiftly decided that of course he *knew* her heart was pounding, because he was so outrageously handsome that he was accustomed to having a whole gaggle of females with pounding hearts following him around dark parking lots. She heaved a ragged sigh and feared for her sanity.

As she climbed into the car, she wondered what the statistics were on gorgeous bankers driving slightly reckless second-grade teachers insane.

Maggie curled up as far away from Adam as possible on her side of the car. Not that it mattered, she thought. Two feet away didn't make him look any less handsome or feel any less devastating. Thank goodness he liked to drive in silence. Coherent speech was beyond her at the moment. With a sense of shock, Maggie realized that having this man's hand on her waist made her feel like a blushing teenager. The absurdity of it would have made her laugh if she hadn't been so alarmed. And now what, Maggie Merriweather? she asked silently.

Sounds of Elvis Presley's "Blue Christmas" filled the car as the Mercedes glided toward Belden. The disc jockeys in Tupelo were fond of playing records by their most famous native son, and at least three times a day during the Christmas season, Elvis could be heard crooning the song.

The gravel on Maggie's driveway crunched under Adam's tires, and silence filled the car after he cut the engine.

Maggie reached for her door handle and spoke over her shoulder. "Thanks for inviting me. Good night, Adam."

"Good night, hell!" he exploded as his hand snaked out to catch her waist and drag her back across the seat.

She turned a startled face up to him and looked into his blazing blue eyes. "What are you doing?" she yelped. "We're not kids on prom night."

Adam threw back his head and roared with laughter. Maggie was thrown completely off balance by his odd behavior. And being off balance made her huffy. "I don't see what's so funny," she said sharply.

"What did you think I was going to do, maul you

in the car?" Adam was still chuckling. "You forgot your coat, Maggie," he finally explained.

It was not news to Maggie; she was always forgetting something. "For that you had to drag me back caveman-style?"

"I've learned to act fast around you. You were going to bail out of my car and leave me shivering out here in the cold, dying for lack of a little hot tea, while you slammed the door in my face." He put on such a mournful expression that Maggie laughed.

"Idiot," she chided him. "Come on in." She was still laughing as she opened her door. "What some men will do for a cup of tea!"

Adam tossed his overcoat onto Maggie's sofa, and she noticed that he was carrying the print of the bufflehead ducks in his hands. Raising her eyebrows in puzzlement, she walked into her kitchen to put the water on to boil. She turned the heat under the copper teapot up to medium high and rejoined Adam.

He was standing in the middle of the den, holding the print in his hands and assessing the room. He turned when she walked in. "Do you have a hammer and nails?"

"What do you intend to do? Crucify me?" she skirted around Adam and sat on the sofa next to his coat. Her hand absently reached out to smooth a wrinkle from the sleeve. The fabric felt rough and tweedy and very masculine to her touch.

"I can assure you, ma'am, my intentions are entirely honorable." He winked at her. "I think this print would be perfect over the mantel. What do you think?"

The impact of what he was saying hit her. Surely he did not intend to give her the print? Accepting such an expensive gift from Adam was out of the question. She pretended not to understand his meaning. "I'm not familiar with your house, so I have no idea whether the print would look good over your mantel."

"Your mantel, Maggie," he corrected her. "The print is my way of apologizing for the boorish conduct of a few people tonight. I did not intend the WI banquet to be an inquisition for you."

"I believe you, Adam," she said solemnly. And it was true; she did believe him. While she certainly didn't approve of his hunting, she had spent enough time with him to know that he was not mean-spirited. "You're not responsible for their conduct, but I still cannot accept your gift."

"Why not? This is the twentieth century, Maggie. Surely you don't still believe that when a lady accepts a gift from a gentleman she is beholden to him?" His mouth was turned up at the corners in amusement.

Maggie laughed in spite of herself. "Beholden? That's quite an old-fashioned word. I haven't heard it since I was five."

"An old-fashioned word to go with old-fashioned notions. Where's the hammer, Maggie?"

"You haven't heard a word I said. I can't possibly accept such an expensive gift." Maybe accepting the gift wouldn't make her "beholden" to Adam, but having it hanging on her wall would be a constant reminder of him. She didn't need that.

"The proper response is 'thank you.' Where are your manners?" The words were spoken lightly, but there was steely determination in his voice. Adam walked to the mantel and held the picture against the wallpaper. The warm, subtle tints of the print looked perfect with Maggie's Williamsburg wallpaper.

"Adam," Maggie protested.

"Maggie," he said firmly. "The hammer." His blue eyes won her over to his will.

Maggie rose from the sofa. "I really shouldn't, but I do love the print, Adam. Thank you."

He grinned triumphantly as she went to the kitchen to get the hammer and nails. Returning to the den, she walked over to the fireplace and climbed up on the hearth. "Where shall I put the nail? Hold the picture up here, Adam."

Adam moved behind her and reached his arms around her on either side, holding the print in front of them both. Maggie was extremely conscious of his nearness and hoped that she wouldn't pound the nail through her hand.

"I would offer to drive the nail, but then I would be up there and you would be down here," Adam murmured behind her. He moved closer, so that his chest was pressed into her back and his arms were touching the length of hers. "I like it better this way."

Maggie's hands shook as she aimed the hammer. Picture-hanging had never been so disturbing. She rapped the nail lightly, and it sank into the wall. It was a good thing he couldn't see her face, she thought suddenly. She was probably moony-eyed and frothing at the mouth. "I know where the picture goes now. You can move back."

Adam didn't move an inch. "And miss all the fun?" he growled.

Maggie tapped the hammer harder than she meant to, driving the nail completely into the wall. Muttering to herself, she used the claw end to pull the nail back out. With Adam standing back there making her hotter than fireworks on the Fourth of July, it was a wonder she hadn't driven the nail clear to Tupelo. "There. That should do it."

Without a word, Adam hung the picture on the nail. The silence in the room was palpable. Maggie held her breath, waiting for him to step back and view their handiwork. But he still stood behind her, holding his arms around her and leaning lightly against her back.

The clock on the mantel ticked loudly, filling the

silent room and marking off the passing minutes, but the two of them stood suspended in time. In slow motion, Adam turned her in his arms. Maggie looked down into his face and saw passion and desire written there. With a dreamlike movement she lowered her lips to his. Softly, gently, her lips moved across his mouth, savoring their familiar warmth.

Still clinging to her, Adam lifted her from the raised hearth and slid her down his body until her feet were touching the floor. Her arms wove around his neck, and rational thought flew from her mind like dandelions before the wind. She was aware only of the delicious way his hard, muscular body was touching hers and the way his lips rekindled the flame that had been burning in her ever since they'd met in the woods. The flame flickered to life and became a blazing conflagration as his tongue explored the warm inner caverns of her mouth.

The kiss deepened as Adam's hands moved down the small of her back, cupping her buttocks and moving her in tightly against his body. She groaned when his lips left hers and moved in a scorching line down the side of her throat. Her head dropped back on the slender column of her neck, letting her magnificent mane of hair sweep backward like a golden curtain.

"Maggie, Maggie," he cried hoarsely. Dimly she heard the metallic whisper as Adam opened the long zipper in the back of her dress. His hands gently pushed the white wool away, his lips searing across one creamy shoulder, then stopping to linger briefly on the small pulse at the base of her throat.

Maggie wound her fingers into his dark hair and pressed his head closer to her willing flesh. Adam's tongue left a burning trail as he moved across to her other shoulder and downward to the tops of her throbbing breasts.

"Lord, I want you, Maggie," he said huskily. She was only dimly aware of being lifted and carried to the sofa. Adam lowered her to the cushions and sank down on top of her. In the dim light of the room, his eyes were so dark they were almost black, as they memorized the lines of her face, her throat, her barely exposed breasts. "You are so beautiful," he whispered hoarsely as he lowered his head once again to claim her lips.

His hands molded her trim hips to his lower body, pulling her hard against the evidence of his desire. Mindlessly she loosened his shirt from the waistband of his pants and slid her hands across the smooth muscles of his back. His skin was smooth-textured and sleek. Maggie let her fingertips trail across his back, reveling in the feel of him. He felt so right, and she wanted him with a fierce intensity that shocked her.

Her body was heavy with need, filled with a molten liquid that coursed through her veins, burning away any lingering thoughts of resistance. She felt his weight shift as Adam sat up to gaze at her. Fierce desire burned in the eyes that roamed her body. He lifted her hand and pressed hot kisses on the tips of each of her fingers. "Maggie, my tigress," he groaned between kisses. "My wild, willful Maggie."

He lowered his head to the inviting crevice between her breasts and planted warm, moist kisses there. Maggie writhed under him, barely aware of the ridges of the sofa cushions against her back and the scratchy feel of Adam's coat against her cheek. "I will tame you, my tigress," he murmured into the soft swells of her breasts.

Something inside Maggie pulled back at his words. Suddenly she was aware of the shrilling of the teapot from the kitchen. Tame her? her mind shouted. *Tame* her? She stiffened, and shoved against his chest with all her strength.

Adam sat upright and looked at her, puzzled. "Maggie?"

She jerked her dress back up over her shoulders. "Not while I have breath in my body," she snapped.

Adam reached down to cup her chin with his hand. "Maggie, what's wrong?"

She swatted at the hand as if it were a pesky fly. "I've come to my senses." She raked a hand through her hair, pushing it back from her hot face.

"I don't understand your sudden mood change." He reached out to smooth back a stray curl from Maggie's forehead. "I have protection, if that's what's worrying you."

"Oh, you do, do you?" she said furiously. "So you planned this 'taming' in advance?"

"Damn." He sprang up from the sofa. "Do you think I could ever plan what happened between us?" He towered over her, scowling.

Maggie glowered up at him. "Didn't you?" she accused.

"You have the memory of an elephant and the tenacity of a bulldog." Leaving her lying tumbled and unfulfilled on the sofa, Adam walked toward the door. A cold blast of air chilled the room when he opened the door. Turning, he spoke softly. "See you in the fighting arena, Maggie." And then he was gone.

Clutching her dress around her, Maggie sat up. Her heart was thundering in her chest and her body was limp with the aftermath of passion. She tucked her legs under her and leaned her head against the sofa back. If she could only get her aroused and throbbing body to move, she would find something to throw against the wall. "That . . . that *hunter!*" she ground out between clenched jaws.

The clock on the mantel ticked loudly and the teapot screamed for attention in the kitchen.

Maggie ignored them both as she sat on the sofa trying to put herself back together again. Outside the wind howled around her windows in December fury. The sound was mournful and vaguely satisfying to Maggie. It matched her mood.

At last she rose from the sofa. Glancing down, she saw Adam's topcoat lying in a rumpled heap against the cushions. The well-organized banker, self-appointed tamer of Maggie Merriweather, had forgotten his coat. She smiled a small, triumphant smile as she walked from the den.

Seven

The sun shining through her bedroom window awakened Maggie. She rolled over in her tangled knot of covers and groaned. She didn't want to wake up, for waking meant remembering last night, and remembering brought a strange kind of hurt.

Opening one eye, which was still gritty from too little sleep, she peered at the new day. Everything looked normal: the sun beamed through her sheer, cream-colored ruffled curtains, bounced off her brass bed, and illuminated the framed pictures of her family. But everything was far from normal, and Maggie Merriweather knew it. She was frighteningly close to being in love with her enemy.

Heaving a resigned sigh, she sat up in the middle of her bed, wrapping the blanket around her shoulders to ward off the chill. She propped her elbows on her knees and her chin in her cupped hands and stared morosely at the ceiling. How could it have happened? she railed mentally. Of all the men in the world, why did it have to be Adam Trent? A *hunter,* for Pete's sake!

Falling in love with him would be so easy, Maggie knew. He had a kind of personal magnetism that was hard to resist. Forgetting him would not be easy. But she could, and she had to. She and Adam were poles apart in everything except their passion for each other. He was accustomed to organization and statistics and decorous behavior. Especially decorous behavior, she thought, and grimaced. Everything she did was madly impulsive and totally unpredictable. She was not decorous at all.

Maggie sprang from the bed, grabbed her robe, and headed to the kitchen. In her den, Adam's coat lay on the sofa and Adam's picture hung on the wall. Her steps slowed, started up again, and finally halted. Adam was everywhere. He was lounging against the sofa cushions laughing about his old second-grade teacher, leaning against the mantel watching the fire, standing in the doorway chiding her about the tea. Oh, Lord, she anguished, forgetting him was going to be harder than she'd thought.

Grabbing the coat off the sofa, she flung it into the hall closet and slammed the door shut. Satisfied that she had at least done that much, she marched to the kitchen, determination ringing in her steps. She banged open the cabinets with unnecessary vigor, grabbed a plastic Snoopy bowl, and stomped to the refrigerator. Milk sloshed onto the counter as she filled her cereal bowl too full.

Taking the soggy mess to the table, Maggie sat in her chair and brooded. Love was sometimes a hurtful thing. Why did she and Adam have to be so different? Irreconcilable differences, she thought. That was what they had.

The scratching of claws on her kitchen floor announced the arrival of her three dogs. They stood in a row, wagging their tails at Maggie and looking pitifully hungry.

"You poor starving babies. Did you think I was never going to get up this morning?" Leaving her soggy cereal floating in its bowl, she went to the cabinet to get the dog food. "After all, it *is* Saturday," she reminded them as she carried the food toward the kitchen door.

They scurried out before her, through the doggie door, wagging tails and jumping all over in the knowledge that they were going to be fed. Maggie smiled as she followed them to the carport. "Such high spirits you guys have. I wish they were catching!"

But they weren't. Not even a phone call to her dad and a beautiful church service on Sunday lifted the gloom that had settled over her when she realized the full extent of her feelings for Adam. Maggie decided that it was one of the longest weekends she had ever spent, and she was more than happy to be back at school Monday, surrounded by chattering seven-year-olds.

"So? How was the banquet?" Martha Jo asked in the hall between second- and third-period classes.

"Remind me to kill you when I have time." Maggie turned to a sandy-haired urchin entering her room. "No, Jeff. You may not take your dog to reading circle. Leave him in the hall."

Jeff hung his head and scuffed his feet on the floor. "Aw, shucks, Miz Meweweaver. He likes to read."

"In you go, Jeff. You can bring him in for the party."

"What was that all about?" Martha Jo asked when the boy was gone.

"Jeff's parents won't let him have a real pet, so he created an imaginary one. Ralph goes everywhere he goes." She turned to the fantasy pet. "Sit, Ralph."

"I think your vacation is overdue, Maggie," Martha Jo said with a laugh.

"Haven't you heard about teaching?" Maggie quipped. "Insanity comes with the territory."

"I thought it belonged exclusively to banking." Adam Trent stood in the hall, poised and smiling and looking every bit as delicious as Maggie remembered. She didn't know whether to laugh or cry.

"And you must be Adam Trent." Martha Jo stuck out her small hand. "Hi. I'm Martha Jo Peterson. Welcome to Bedlam. You're just the sort of distraction we need today."

Taking Martha Jo's hand, he smiled that smile, the one that always melted Maggie's marshmallow heart and transformed her into a Raggedy Ann without any stuffing. She was so busy getting stiffening back into her legs and starch back into her heart that she didn't hear a word they were saying. All she knew was that suddenly Martha Jo was gone and she was standing alone in the hall with Adam and he was holding her hand and she had to start all over again with the starch. Damn! she thought.

"This is getting to be a habit with me." Adam smiled down at her.

"What is?" Maggie's confusion was genuine. She was so disturbed by seeing him again—particularly after coming to the painful conclusion that she was only a breath away from loving him—that she didn't know what to say.

"Bearing gifts and saying 'I'm sorry.' You must believe that I never intended for you to be stoned at the banquet. So I have brought this as a peace offering." He indicated the enormous tree that trailed down the hall behind him. He held the trunk easily with one hand.

"I would hardly call the few nasty remarks at the banquet a stoning." What happened later on the couch had been a stoning, she wanted to add. She had come away from that encounter bruised and battered. But it would not happen again. The starch hardened in her legs and spread throughout her entire body as she became determined to spurn both the man *and* his tree, a tree she had been wanting for a week for her students' party. "It's too bad you went to all that trouble to bring me a tree. I have twenty-two students inside waiting for a reading lesson." She stepped inside her room, and Adam came in behind her, tree and all.

"Don't mind me. I'll be as quiet as a mouse." Hefting the large cedar tree upright, he carried it to the corner of her room and proceeded to place a stand on the floor and anchor the tree in it. He looked as if he owned the room and everybody in it.

"Is that a Cwis'mas twee, Miz Meweweaver?"

"Can we help decorate it?"

"Fantastic!"

"Who is that man? Is he your husband?"

Maggie knew she had been outfoxed. Her students were bouncing up and down with excitement, and Adam was puttering about the tree humming. *Humming!* He even had the gall to wink at her. "We will not have reading circle today," she announced unnecessarily. "Today we will trim the tree."

Turning her back on all the hubbub, she gathered the handmade ornaments and garlands from the top shelf of her supply closet. Standing on tiptoe, she reached to get the lopsided treetop angel that had fallen to the back.

"Here, let me do that." Adam was suddenly behind her, reaching his arms around her to retrieve the ornament.

Maggie stood very still for a moment, willing herself to ignore the way her blood was sizzling through her veins. "You've done quite enough already," she said stiffly.

His right hand caressed the length of her arm as he dragged the lopsided angel out with his left. "I'm staying to help trim the tree," he said matter-of-factly.

She whirled on him, her eyes blazing. "You haven't been invited." Of all the overbearing, blue-eyed, gorgeous men, he took the cake! she fumed. This was *her* classroom, and she would not let him invade it the way he had invaded her den. Unconsciously, she rubbed the arm he had touched.

"Yes, I have. A little kid named Ralph asked me to stay."

"Ralph?" Maggie's eyes sparkled with suppressed laughter.

"A cute kid with freckles and sandy hair. He seemed sort of bashful. Instead of coming right out and asking me, he said, 'Ralph wants you to stay.'"

"Ralph is his dog." She burst out laughing at the look on Adam's face.

"I might have known you would have animals in your classroom, Maggie. If you're anything, you're unconventional."

She almost didn't tell him about Ralph. Let him think what he wanted, she thought recklessly. Maybe he would decide she was completely off her rocker and stay away. Then she wouldn't have to be bothered about stiffening her spine and stilling her pulse and hardening her heart whenever he was around. It was getting to be an enormous chore. "The little boy is Jeff, and Ralph is a figment of his imagination."

A tiny girl with apple cheeks and flaxen curls bounded up to Adam and took his hand. "Come on, Mr. Merriweather. We're ready to put Phyllis on the tree."

Adam glanced at Maggie in astonishment. "Phyllis?"

"You have her in your left hand." Maggie

laughed. "The treetop angel." Following them to the tree, she pondered the case of mistaken identity. What if she really were Adam's wife? Just thinking about the possibility made her hot all over. It would never happen, of course. Bankers, like nursing-home directors, didn't marry Joan of Arcs. Joan of Arcs stuck out like sore thumbs in staid old banks and snobby country clubs. But most of all there was the matter of the animals. Her heart felt like stone as she stood on the edge of the circle and watched Adam help her students trim the tree.

They adored him. He chatted and laughed with them and took turns holding them up high to trim the top branches of the tree. Maggie even noticed that he had brought a live tree, with its roots balled in burlap for replanting after Christmas. That was exactly what she would have done, she thought with tenderness, and suspicion. Had he done that because of her, or was he genuinely interested in preserving forests?

"Ready for Phyllis, Mr. Merriweather." Adam had not corrected the children's mistaken idea, she noticed.

"I'm afraid I can't reach the top, but your teacher can." Before Maggie realized what was happening, Adam had thrust Phyllis into her hands and had swung her up in his arms. With his strong, gentle hands spanning her waist, he lifted her toward the top of the tree. "Can you reach the top, Maggie?"

With his hands on her, she could have reached the stars, she thought, but she didn't tell him so. She made a strangled sound that vaguely resembled "yes" as she struggled to concentrate on anchoring Phyllis to the treetop. The heady scent of fresh cedar made her light-headed. At least she told herself that was what it was. It took her longer to place the angel than it should have, and Adam was enjoying himself immensely. At last Phyllis was secure. "All through," she announced.

As Adam lowered her to the floor, he whispered. "Call me if you ever need a stepladder. The job has its compensations." He placed a fleeting kiss on her cheek, and it was done so quickly, she wasn't sure it had happened. Except that her cheek still tingled from his touch.

"Remember that you're in school," she scolded him halfheartedly.

"I was always naughty in school."

"Fortunately, you are leaving soon."

"On the contrary. Ralph has invited me to stay for the Christmas 'page nut.' I told him I would." His eyes gleamed at her as he leaned casually against the wall beside the tree. "I'll watch from here. I don't think I would fit into one of your desks."

"I'm going to have to do something about Ralph," she muttered as she marched, heels clicking, to the front of the room. She was aware of Adam's eyes on her as she restored order and assembled the children for their pageant. Each child had a part in the story. Maggie moved to the back of the room with her prompting book as the shepherds and the host of angels took over.

"Behold!" An exuberant voice rang through the room as the second graders began their pageant. Their eyes were round with wonder, and their tiny fists clutched wrinkled slips of paper, their lines in the play.

"I bring you good te . . . t . . ."

"Tidings," Maggie prompted. The fresh green scent of the cedar tree filled her nostrils, and the nearness of Adam filled her heart. She wiped her forehead with the back of her hand.

With a sense of shock, Maggie felt Adam's hand at the back of her neck, underneath her hair. Slowly, he lifted her hair and bent to plant a moist kiss on the nape of her neck. "I love watching you work, Maggie. You were right: you do give a hundred percent to everything you care about," he whispered. "I can't wait to get my hundred percent."

If he had intended to throw her off balance, he had succeeded. "Never," she whispered fiercely. Was it only this morning that she had decided to forget him? Oh, Lord! She moved away from his hand and tried to find her place in the pageant script. Up front, her students were totally engrossed in the play, oblivious to the goings on in the back of the room.

"Maggie," he chided her, "is that any way to talk to an enemy?" The sparkle in his eyes told her that he was enjoying every minute of the devilment he was causing. "After all, it *is* the Christmas season. What do you say we call a truce?"

"The last time we called a truce, I ended up being the whipping boy at your hunters' banquet. You've wasted your time if you came here just to call a truce with me."

"Well, actually," he drawled, "I came here to bed you. But I don't cotton to the idea of having such a large audience. Do you?" He grinned wickedly.

"Barbarian!" she hissed. Where had she ever gotten the idea that he was lovable? He was the devil in disguise!

"Fight me, Tigress." The light of battle gleamed in his eyes. "You want it just as much as I do. We started something the other night that has to be finished."

"Never!" she whispered harshly. "Go away."

"You'll change your mind, Maggie," he promised her, and chuckled softly.

"Not till hell freezes over," she said between clenched teeth.

His arm shot out, pulling her tight against him. His kiss was brief but savage. "You'd be surprised how fast hell can freeze over in Tupelo." Without another word he was gone.

Eight

With his parting words still ringing in her ears and her heart thudding against her ribs like a jackhammer, Maggie tried to find her place in the pageant script. Little Melanie Roscoe was loudly announcing that she would "plunder those things in her heart."

Her eyes followed the words, but her mind flew restlessly back and forth between the present and the immediate past, between her classroom and Adam. Their meetings had taken on a pattern: casual greetings quickly advanced to unleashed passion, which signaled retreat and verbal scrimmaging. It all resembled some ancient ritual, she thought. Her fingers quivered on the lines of the script as she tried to concentrate on the play. Was it a mating ritual? Were she and Adam like the animals who bared their claws and spurned one another before they mated? Maggie's cheeks grew hot at the idea. Her relationship with him had become far more complicated than simply that of hunter and preservationist.

"Miz Meweweaver. We is finished. What do we do now?"

Maggie snapped out of her deep thought. "Are," she corrected automatically. Reluctance slowed her steps as she walked to the front of her room. For the first time in her teaching career, she didn't want to confront the lively, curious faces of her second-graders. She wanted to disappear into the woods with her trumpet and go into battle for her wild friends, free and unfettered by thoughts of Adam Trent. She wanted the two halves of herself to come together so that she was not a divided woman, torn between Adam and her commitment to her cause. But most of all, she wanted Adam. She wanted him so fiercely that her teeth were clenched, making her jaw rigid as she faced her students.

The rest of the day seemed to creep by, so that Maggie was worn to a frazzle when the dismissal bell finally rang. Her usual brisk stride slowed to a crawl as she left the school building and walked to her pickup truck. The sharp December wind stung her cheeks and made her eyes smart. She shivered and pulled her toboggan cap low over her eyes. The sky was murky and dismal. She glanced up at the gray cloud banks, stacked like dirty cotton and moving slowly across the face of the sun. All that dreariness suited her perfectly. Why should the sun shine when she felt so rotten?

Her dogs greeted her with joyous barks and followed her into her warm den. Maggie struck a match to the logs she had placed in the fireplace. The wood hissed and sputtered as the fire caught. Kneeling before the flames, she extended her hands toward the fire. With her dogs lying contentedly on the braided hearth rug beside her and the fire creating a cheery glow in the room, some warmth gradually crept into Maggie's soul. Being surrounded by familiar things always made her feel better.

She sat back on her heels. Even if she and Adam were involved in some ancient love rite, she still had the prerogative of stopping it. The choice was hers. It would always be hers.

The raucous ringing of both the phone and the doorbell interrupted Maggie's solitude. Knowing that she couldn't answer both at the same time, she raced to the phone, picked up the receiver, and yelled in the direction of the door. "Come in!"

Jim Merriweather walked through the door, and Maggie waved him over to the sofa.

"If that's an invitation, I accept." Amusement was evident in Adam Trent's voice.

Maggie looked at the phone as if she wanted to kill it. Adam was the last person in the world she wanted to talk to. "Not you," she said sharply. "My brother just walked through the door. Hello, Adam." She hoped her voice was sufficiently dripping with icicles to discourage him. "Please be brief."

"I called to invite you to go hunting with me."

"You must be out of your mind."

Jim Merriweather raised dark brows over green eyes that crinkled with mirth at the corners. Interlacing his long fingers behind his head, he winked at his sister. "Go get 'em, Maggie."

"Don't tell me you went to all that trouble to get a permit and don't intend to use it."

Maggie grinned with delight. Her little scheme with the nursing-home residents had paid off. What was more, she could tell that Adam wasn't too happy with the results. "You can mark that on the scoreboard. One for me, zero for you."

"Are we keeping score, Maggie?" His voice was scathing. "If I had known that, perhaps I could have put something on the scoreboard for last Friday night. One for me and one for you. A standoff."

For a moment, all the intensity of the emotions she had felt that night on the sofa swept over Maggie. A standoff. Had it been that, or just another phase of the mating rites? A knot of uncertainty formed in her stomach, and she had to clear her throat before she could speak. "There's always a score in battle, Adam. A winner and a loser. I don't intend to lose."

"Neither do I." The way he said it made her shiver. Were they talking about the same battle? she wondered.

Jim was sitting forward on the sofa, his lively green eyes dancing with excitement as he cheered his sister on. He had been out of town, buying cattle for his farm, and had no idea what particular cause Maggie was fighting for now; but, knowing her, he was sure that she was up to her feisty little neck in trouble.

Maggie threw a look at her brother, pleading for moral support. Jim winked at her and made the victory sign with his fingers.

"Tell me, Adam, do I know any of the other recipients of the hunting permits? We *are* talking about antlerless deer season, aren't we?"

"You know damned well that's what we're talking about. How do these names grab you? Emma Vinson and Fannie Mae Clark."

Maggie was so pleased with the success of her venture that she laughed aloud. "That's wonderful!"

"I would say it's just short of illegal, Maggie, stuffing boxes like that." There was a slight pause. "That *is* what you did, isn't it?"

"I never reveal my battle tactics, even after the battle is won."

"So we're back to that." The sound that came over the phone was very much akin to an exasperated sigh. "Have you ever considered what it would be like between us if you lowered the banner and just let things take their natural course?"

She had considered it until she was frazzled from the effort. But lengthy consideration did nothing to change the facts, and she knew it. They had basic philosophical differences that could not be resolved. There was no point in admitting that to Adam, though. He had never said a thing about love, had probably never spent a sleepless night wanting her. His only admitted interest was working to thwart her cause by taming her. And that included his latest avowed intention of bedding her.

"I'll never lower the banner, Adam."

"We'll see about that, Maggie."

The dead receiver buzzed in her hand. He had hung up. She stood clutching the receiver until her knuckles were white. Damn Adam Trent! She felt as if she had been run through a meat grinder.

Replacing the receiver, she turned to her brother and held out her arms. He bounded over and scooped her up for a bear hug.

Her voice was muffled against his shoulder. "When did you get back?"

"Late last night. It was a hell of a trip, with the cattle I bought bawling all the way home from Texas, and a blowout near Jackson that damn near caused me to wreck the truck." He set her on her feet and pulled her down beside him on the sofa. "What was that all about?" He nodded in the direction of the phone.

"You heard?"

"Hell, Sis, how could I help it? I was sitting right here."

Maggie raked her hand through her long hair and leaned her head against the back of the sofa. Of course he had heard, she thought. That was how messed up her mind had been ever since she'd met Adam Trent. "You know about FOA. The man on the other end of the phone was a hunter."

"Come on, Maggie. This is your brother you're talking to. From the way you were acting, I'd say the man on the other end of the phone is much more than just a hunter." Jim lifted his tall frame from the sofa. "Got any coffee around here, Maggie?"

"If I had known you were coming I would have bought some on the way home from school. Sorry about that. Just tea." Jim was right about Adam's being more than just a hunter. But then, he had always been able to read her like a book. Even when they were kids he'd been able to read her moods more quickly than Dad.

Jim walked to the fireplace and leaned against the mantel. "When are you going to start keeping a man's drink around here?" He always said that, and his lazy smile told her that, as usual, he was just teasing.

Standing against the mantel, her brother looked relaxed and casual. Maggie began to hope that he had lost interest in her phone conversation.

She should have known better. "You didn't tell me about the man, Sis." The look he gave her was a penetrating one.

Maggie sighed. She had never lied to Jim, and didn't plan to start now. "The man is Adam Trent, and he gets under my skin the way no man ever has. But he's a hunter, dammit. And that spoils everything."

Jim let out a low whistle. "I'm sorry, Maggie. What rotten luck."

"Oh, Jim," she said with a wail. "What am I going to do? I've fought this thing until I'm sick and tired of fighting. I just can't reconcile myself to being halfway in love with a man who hunts."

"Halfway?"

"I don't know, Jim. I just don't know." She

jumped up from the sofa and came to join him beside the fire. The conflict was evident in her turbulent green eyes. "What am I going to do?"

"I'm afraid I can't advise you about love, Sis. My track record in that department is not too good. Fell in love with Jenny Lou Davis when I was sixteen, and she turned out to be the town tart. It broke my heart so bad I just gave up." He grinned sheepishly. Maybe a little foolishness would lighten Maggie's mood, he thought.

Maggie knew what he was doing. He had always been able to tease her out of the doldrums. But not this time. "A lot of help you are," she scoffed.

Jim turned serious. "I wish to hell I could help you. I've never seen you this worked up. Not even when Mac dumped you."

Maggie punched him lightly on the arm. "Thanks, I needed that. Don't you know, you big oaf, a girl doesn't like to be reminded that she was jilted?"

Taking both her hands between his work-roughened, farmer's hands, Jim looked into her eyes. "All I know, Sis, is that you have to be true to yourself. You've never quit paddling in midstream, and I can't imagine you doing that now. Why, ever since we were kids and you used to come crying home to Dad, clutching a bird with a broken wing in your hands, you've fought and spit and scratched for the animals." He squeezed her hands warmly between his.

Maggie shut her eyes against the tears that were threatening to spill. How she loved her brother! She took a deep breath and opened her eyes. "What do you say the two of us run up to Bill's Quick Stop and get a jar of instant coffee?"

"Make that a can of the real stuff and you're on." Jim released her hands and grabbed his plaid wool coat. "I'm driving, Maggie," he announced as they walked side by side out the door. "You drive like a bat out of hell."

Jim stayed for supper, and by the time he left, Maggie was feeling considerably better. Her brother's unfailing good humor, as he sat in her den downing cups of real coffee and spinning anecdotes about his Texas cattle-buying trip, put her problems with Adam in their proper perspective.

The bounce returned to Maggie's step, and she was so caught up in the hectic pace of school as they prepared to recess for Christmas vacation that she was able to dismiss Adam from her mind. Except when she looked at the tree. At odd moments, she would catch herself staring at the lopsided angel perched among the cedar branches. And then she would close her eyes, trying without success to shut him out.

The day school was let out, Maggie stood in the middle of her empty classroom and wondered what she would do for the next two weeks. Time had never hung heavy on her hands before, but now she felt a driving need to be busy. To be so busy that she could blot out everything that had happened between her and Adam.

Martha Jo was going to Aspen on a ski trip, her dad was taking a senior citizens' Christmas cruise, and Jim was busy with his farm. She roamed restlessly through her house for two days, swiping at specks of dust hidden behind her porcelain animal collection and scrubbing her bathroom tiles until they gleamed. She rifled through a stack of books she had intended to read when she had time, but now that she had time, she found she had lost interest.

She felt suspended on the edge of time, waiting for something to happen. Finally she could stand it no longer. She poured a week's supply of dog food into the pet-food dispenser, scattered plenty of shelled corn for her ducks, and bundled herself up in a pair of scruffy old army fatigues, a wool plaid shirt, and her puffy parka. Pulling her toboggan cap down low, she grabbed her trumpet case and headed for her pickup.

The cold engine choked and died, sputtered and caught, and Maggie sat on the seat filled with exhilaration. She didn't have any idea where she was going; she only knew that she was going *somewhere* and going to do *something*, even if it was the wrong thing. She patted the horn case beside her reassuringly and screeched out of her driveway.

She clipped down McCullough Boulevard, past Bill's Quick Stop, past the Belden Post Office, and past the new truck stop that sprawled across a barren hill. Chimes from the Belden Baptist Church tower rang out the glorious season as Maggie made a left turn onto Highway 78. She leaned over and flipped on the radio as she was passing Payne's Fish and Steak House in Sherman, then rode, tapping time to the music on her steering wheel and humming.

By the time she reached New Albany and had turned left onto Highway 30, Maggie knew that she was headed into Tallahatchie River bottom. She reached over and touched her trumpet case. "Like Jim said, I don't quit paddling in the middle of the stream." The sound of her own voice gave her a sense of purpose. She was headed into the woods to foil the hunters. And that was all. Certain dark-haired, blue-eyed bankers didn't enter into this matter at all.

That was what Maggie was still telling herself fifteen miles later, when the weatherman interrupted the music to warn travelers of an approaching snowstorm. "It looks like a big one," he said excitedly. "If this thing develops, it could outdo the snow we had in 'seventy-five."

Maggie smiled. Weathermen in the South were always getting worked up over snow. Nine times out of ten it never came, and when it did, the few pitiful snowflakes that barely wet the hoods of cars could hardly be called a snow. Big snows were as rare as hen's teeth down South. That was why, when they did come, southerners were always unprepared.

The pine thickets of Holly Springs National Forest loomed ahead, and Maggie felt a sense of excitement as she neared the river. The gravel road was mushy from recent rains, and Maggie's tires slipped to the left. Fighting with the wheel and muttering under her breath, she came around the bend to the river. Her brakes squealed in protest as she whirled off the road and stopped.

When she stepped down from her truck, the cold wind hit her with a blast that made her teeth chatter. She had forgotten her gloves, so she jammed her hands into her pockets as she walked along the riverbank to see what was going on. There were no sounds—no popping of guns, no honking of ducks, nothing except the gentle sighing of pine boughs in the wind.

She squatted on her heels and waited. Thirty minutes later, with her nose turned red and her feet nearly frozen, she walked back to her truck. Gratefully she climbed into the cab, turned the key, and put the pickup in reverse. Her tires spun with a sluggish, muddy sound.

Maggie bailed out to see her rear tires sunk almost to the axle in mud. "Damn," she said. She dragged some fallen branches under the tires and tried once more to back out. The same ominous whirring greeted her efforts.

She jumped down and glared at the mess. "Of all the rotten luck." She lifted her leg and kicked the tires in sheer frustration.

"I don't think that will do any good, Maggie."

She whirled around to see Adam standing at the edge of the forest, under a huge cottonwood tree, his gun unbreached and slung over his shoulder. She could have spit nails. "I don't need any advice from you," she snapped.

He grinned. "You need more than advice. You need help." He sauntered casually toward her, his buckskin coat unsnapped and swinging away from his trim-fitting jeans in a way that made Maggie's mouth go dry. He noticed the direction her eyes were looking, and his grin got even bigger.

Her face flaming, Maggie whirled back around and kicked her tires again. "Crazy barbarian."

She heard him behind her, opening her pickup door and putting his gun inside. His voice was muffled inside the cab when he spoke. "I see you decided to come hunting after all." He was referring, she knew, to her horn.

"Hunting for hunters," she said fiercely. She wanted to strangle him for being the one to come along to pull her out of the mud, *and* for being so damned smug about it!

"And what do you intend to do with me now that you've found me?" He had come up behind her so quietly she had not heard him. She jumped.

Whirling around, hands on hips, she faced him angrily. "Certainly not to bed you." The minute she said it, she could have kicked herself all the way back to Belden.

Adam looked at her blazing face, tipped back his head, and laughed. "I must have made a bigger impression than I thought." His blue eyes sparkled with humor as he baited her.

"You didn't make any impression at all, you muleheaded money-changer!" She shoved at his chest with both hands. "Move out of my way. I'm leaving." She bounded around him and slammed into her pickup.

"Maggie!" Adam called to her over the loud revving of her engine. Her tires spun uselessly, slinging mud in every direction as she stubbornly gave her truck the gas.

Tears of frustration stung her cheeks as she finally released the gas pedal and pounded her fists against the wheel. "Oh, damn," she wailed. "Why did it have to be him?"

The door jerked open, and Adam reached in and yanked her out of the seat. "I ought to turn you over my knee and spank you." Globs of black mud clung to his face and clothes. "What in the hell do you think you're doing?" He gripped both her arms as he towered over her, scowling.

"Let go of me!" she demanded.

He tightened his hold, hauling her up against his chest. Her chin brushed against his soft chamois shirt as she tilted her head up to look defiantly into his eyes. "Not until you quit fighting me, so we can get you out of the mud," he said.

"I don't need you," she muttered as she struggled against him. She felt her boots slipping on the slick ground. Her feet did a wild dance, fighting for purchase in the mud.

Adam held her arms, trying to steady her, but his own feet lost ground as Maggie fell heavily against him, propelling them both backward. They had been standing on the edge of the sloping riverbank, and now they teetered uncertainly, feet scrabbling in the slippery earth. Adam grabbed at the low-hanging branch of a spindly willow tree and missed. He tipped over backward, and Maggie toppled with him.

Together they rolled down the embankment, legs tangled with legs, arms locked, gaining momentum as they went. Mud slicked their clothes and clung to their hair as their bodies pitched against each other's. Maggie was conscious of broken twigs and prickly grass against her back. But most of all she was conscious of muscular thighs and a broad expanse of chest and a face pressed so close she could see a faint shadow of beard stubble.

They hit the water with a splat. Maggie lay solidly against Adam's chest, the icy water lapping at her clothes, and mud caked in her hair. "Oh, you . . . you . . ." she sputtered. The water that had splashed into her face made small black rivers of the mud caked there.

Adam sat up in the shallow water, pulling Maggie with him. He shook the water from his hair, looked at her face, and roared with laughter. "You ought to see your face." The whole situation struck him as ludicrous, and he sat in the Tallahatchie River chuckling.

"You mule! We're going to freeze to death in the river and you sit there laughing." Reaching into the river, she scooped up a handful of slime. With deliberation, she leaned over and smeared his face. "Now you should see yours."

Adam struggled up from the water, his buckskin jacket hanging heavily and his jeans molded to his skin. He jerked Maggie up from the water and quickly divested her of her sopping parka. "Come on," he said between chattering teeth.

"What are you doing? I'm not going anywhere with you." She planted her feet in the river and glared at him.

"You're the one who didn't want to freeze to death, but if you've changed your mind, I'll go without you." Unceremoniously he hauled her out of the river and half-dragged her back up the slick bank.

She shivered as the sharp wind bit through her wet clothes. "Where are we going?" They surely couldn't go anywhere in her truck. It was still stuck in the mud.

"My hunting cabin is less than half a mile from here. We can make it." He shucked his heavy jacket and put it, along with her parka, into her pickup.

Then he turned and wrapped his right arm around a shivering Maggie.

She started to protest through quivering lips, but he cut her off. "Body heat. We'll have to walk fast, Maggie. Put your arms around me and stay close."

With Adam setting the pace, they walked rapidly through the forest. Their wet boots slogged and squished as Maggie's long legs matched his stride.

"Adam . . ."

"Don't talk. You need all your wind for walking. We should be there in less than ten minutes if we can keep up this pace."

The wind sliced into them, and Maggie hid her face in the lee of Adam's shoulder for protection from its icy blast. He pulled her closer, and, through their wet clothes, she could feel a faint warmth from his body.

When Maggie had decided that she could go no farther, that she would just sit down on a log and turn to a lump of ice, they came upon the cabin. Set among the lush forest of pine and cedar, its weather-grayed cypress walls and wooden shingles seemed to blend in with the trees. Beside the front door stood two enormous cottonwood trees, their limbs bare of leaves and their silver-white trunks gleaming in the afternoon shadows.

Spurred on by the welcome sight, Maggie and Adam ran the remaining few yards to the front door. The heavy wooden door squeaked on its hinges as they stepped inside the cabin.

Maggie hugged her arms around herself and shivered as Adam began stripping off his clothes. Although there was no fire inside the cabin, it felt like an oven, compared to the frigid temperature outside.

She heard Adam's boots hit the floor with a thud and then watched with fascination as he unbuttoned his chamois shirt and slid it from his shoulders. A fine pelt of dark hair covered his chest and came to a V at the top of his waistband.

She bit her blue lips to stop the chattering of her teeth as she watched his hands move to his belt buckle. Good grief! she thought. He was going to strip buck naked while she stood there and gawked like a sixteen-year-old. Blushing, she turned her back on him and looked for something to wrap around herself.

"Good Lord, woman," Adam bellowed, "don't just stand there. Strip!"

Her head shot up, and their eyes clashed. His hands hovered near his belt buckle, and his voice held a veiled threat when he spoke again. "Are you going to get undressed or shall I do it for you?"

Nine

"You wouldn't dare!" Maggie answered furiously.

Adam's eyebrows shot up over his extraordinary eyes. "Oh, wouldn't I?" he asked softly. He took a step in her direction.

Her eyes widened in panic. Good Lord, he meant it. "Where?" she asked, scanning the room for a place to strip out of her wet clothes. The room they were in had been designed for cooking, sleeping, and eating. There seemed to be no escape from Adam's eyes.

"Through there." Adam's nod indicated a door that Maggie's panic-stricken eyes had missed. Shivering, she hurried in that direction.

The door led to a large bathroom that was meant to be strictly functional. The cypress walls had been coated with sealer and left their natural color. There was a full towel rack on one wall, and a mirror big enough for a man to see his face while shaving.

Maggie leaned over and pulled off her wet boots,

and then her nerveless fingers fumbled with the buttons on her sodden shirt. "Damn," she muttered as they resisted her efforts to pop them open.

"Need any help in there?" Adam called cheerfully through the door.

Maggie's head snapped up. "No!" She cocked her ear to the door, listening. What was he up to? she wondered. Would he come barging through the door to undress her as another one of his taming tactics? She heard a metallic clunk as his belt buckle hit the floor. Her face flushed hot at the idea of Adam standing on the other side of the door in just his underwear.

With a guilty start, she backed away from the door and struggled out of her wet clothes. What did it matter to her if he was standing out there naked? She flung her wet army pants into the corner and stripped off her panties and bra. She was in a real huff by the time she got into the shower.

She slathered herself with soap and scrubbed away the mud. The hot water stung her skin's chilled surface, and the faintly spicy smell of soap rose in the steam of the shower. It was a man's soap, she thought. His soap. She stood for a second, the soap poised in midair. Adam had stood in this same spot, massaging this same soap into that magnificent chest of his. Maggie closed her eyes and let the fragrance drift around her.

"You can put this on when you've finished."

Maggie nearly jumped out of her skin. He was there in the bathroom with her! From the sound of his voice, he was standing right outside the shower door, the smoky glass door that would have perfectly silhouetted her body for his viewing. She swallowed a lump in her throat and stood still under the rush of water.

The seconds crawled slowly by, and at last she heard his footsteps and then the slamming of the bathroom door. Cautiously she opened the shower door a crack and peeked around the corner. A large shirt in apple-green chamois was lying on the vanity. She hastily finished her shower. She didn't want to be in there a minute longer than she had to, with Adam roaming in and out at will.

Maggie stepped out of the shower and toweled herself dry. Then, wrapping the towel around her wet hair, she put on Adam's shirt. The shirttail came to mid-thigh, but even so, she noted, she'd have to be careful, for the only underwear she had lay in a soggy heap on the floor.

She opened the bathroom door cautiously, half expecting to see Adam parading around stark naked. Instead, he was bending over the fireplace in a pair of dry jeans, coaxing the freshly laid fire to life.

"That fire looks wonderful," Maggie said as she crossed the room. She noticed that Adam had managed to wash the mud off his face while she'd been showering.

He glanced across his shoulder at her, and his eyebrows rose. "That's a definite improvement."

"Getting rid of the mud helped."

"I'm not talking about the mud. I'm talking about my shirt. It looks better with you in it."

Maggie knelt in front of the fire and extended her hands. It would be best to ignore that comment. The situation was volatile enough already. "Hmm, that feels good." Maggie took the towel from her hair and began to massage its wet strands. The blaze from the fire cast a red glow across her cheeks and gilded her exposed legs with gold.

The fire spit and crackled as Adam watched her in silence. Abruptly, he stood up and stomped across the room.

Startled, Maggie looked up. "Where are you going?"

"To take a shower. I could get twenty years for

what I'm thinking." The bathroom door banged shut behind him.

Maggie sank back on the thick-piled rug and stretched out her legs. "Whew!" It was a good thing Adam had left, she thought. If he had stayed a minute longer, there was no telling what she might have done. Sitting half-naked with him in front of a cozy fire in a cabin deep in the woods revived all the sexual tension between them. And where Adam was concerned, it didn't take much to do that.

While he was in the shower, Maggie gazed around the room. The bed dominated one corner. It was a cherry-wood four-poster, covered with a brightly colored quilt. An eighteenth-century gateleg table made of cedar and cypress stood in the center of the room. Two cane-bottom chairs stood beside the table, and two more flanked the fireplace. Adam obviously loved antique furniture and had spared no expense in furnishing his cabin.

The corner of the room opposite the bed had been furnished as a kitchen, and Maggie noticed that he had rigged the sink into an oak washstand. With its natural cypress walls and antique furnishings, there was a true flavor of early Americana in the cabin. Being here was almost like being transported backward in time, she mused.

The opening of the bathroom door caused Maggie to jump. Hastily she tucked her legs under her.

Adam chuckled. "What's the matter, Maggie—afraid I'll eat you?" He strode across the room and sat back on his heels on the hearth rug. The fire glistened on droplets of water clinging to his bare chest. His dark hair was still damp and tousled across his forehead.

No, afraid I'll eat you, Maggie thought. "Of course not," she said firmly.

"By the way, I rinsed your underthings and hung them in the bathroom to dry."

"You did *what?*"

"Unless you'd prefer to go '*au naturel*' while you're here with me." He kept a straight face, but his eyes sparkled with humor. "The rest of your clothes will require a little more attention, I'm afraid."

Her face flushed at the idea of Adam's performing such an intimate chore for her. Ever since he had stepped out of the forest to rescue her, the situation had been spiraling out of control. Maggie felt herself being irrevocably pulled into the bright web of passion that had already ensnared them in its subtle threads. Her only defense was anger.

"How dare you, you . . . you Peeping Tom! First you dump me into the Tallahatchie River and now you maul my—"

"Panties." He grinned at her.

"You keep out of this!" she yelled, jumping to her feet. "You've been nothing but trouble ever since I met you. You and your gun-toting, animal-slaughtering tactics."

"Maggie," he warned her.

"And giving interviews behind my back just because you're some hotshot banker!" Maggie was on a roll now. "Sneaking around in a Santa Claus suit, fooling little old ladies. Well, you can't fool me."

Adam was on his feet beside her. His arm snaked out and brought her against his body with a soft whump. "Are you finished?" His voice was tight as their eyes met.

"No, you bar—" His mouth stopped her words. Fiercely his lips pressed against hers, goaded by the anger that crackled in the air around them.

Maggie tried to steel herself against him, to resist her overwhelming hunger for his touch. His tongue pushed impatiently against her closed lips, and his hands cupped her bare buttocks, hauling her hard against his lean hips.

Maggie was powerless against the passionate assault. Her arms circled his shoulders as her lips responded to his demands. The desire that had been simmering between them since that icy day in Boguefala Bottom exploded.

Adam groaned deep in his throat as his anger turned to intense need. His hands reached up and popped the buttons of her shirt as he impatiently tore it aside. Her nipples, erect and throbbing, pressed against his chest, and from a long way off Maggie heard the buttons as they pinged to the floor one by one. His tongue sent hot thrills through her as his mouth came down and covered her straining nipples.

Adam lowered her to the deep-piled rug, and her hair made a bright fan as it streamed behind her in the firelight. Their eyes locked for a moment, burning with the awareness of their shared passion. "Lord, you don't know how long I've wanted this," Adam said huskily, and Maggie heard his belt buckle hit the floor somewhere behind him.

Her arms yearned upward, imploring him to relieve the raging fire that consumed her. His body lowered over hers, and he took her fiercely, wildly. Behind them, the fire cast an other-world glow over the timeless dance their bodies performed. All their pent-up passions exploded in a release that shook them to the core.

Adam lay still atop her, nuzzling her sweat-dampened brow with his lips. "Maggie," he breathed. "Oh, my Lord, Maggie."

Her arms tightened around him, crushing him to her breasts. Their loving had felt like coming home to Maggie, and now she *knew*. There were no halfways and nearlys and almosts with Adam. She could no longer kid herself. She was in love with him, completely and irrevocably.

Tears trembled on the tips of her lashes, and she blinked to keep them from spilling over. Everything about this love was impossible, but she would hold him just a little while longer. She wrapped her arms tighter around Adam.

"Hey, Maggie." Adam lifted his head and gave her a lopsided grin. "Not so tight." Seeing the glistening of tears in her eyes, his teasing quickly changed to concern. He shifted his weight off her and propped himself up on his elbow at her side. One hand gently brushed across her eyelashes. "What's wrong?"

"Everything."

"No, it's not. I love you, Maggie."

"But—"

His fingers pressed softly against her lips. "Let me finish. I've fought it for a long time. I kept telling myself that I would make you pay for spoiling my hunts and bringing havoc to my bank, to my life. But every time I came near you, I ended up wanting you in my arms. I think I've loved you since that first time I saw you, so cocksure and gorgeous, riding that boat in the Tallahatchie River and tooting that damned horn."

She gave him a tremulous smile. "It's not a damned horn; it's a silver trumpet."

He lifted the hand that lay between them and kissed the tips of her fingers. Maggie's heart melted as she looked up at him. The firelight gilded his sun-bronzed skin and danced in his remarkable blue eyes.

Outside the cabin the wind moaned beneath its heavy load of snow and finally dropped its burden like a white blanket over the earth. The snow blew down over the trees and drifted over the bushes and sifted down on the windowsills. It covered the ground in a deep carpet, hiding the roads and banking along the roadsides.

Inside the cabin, Maggie and Adam were too

absorbed in each other to know the capricious trick nature had played on the South.

Shivers scattered along her spine as Adam continued his slow, lazy kissing of her hand. His lips moved across the palm, skimmed the wrist, and inched upward to plant a warm, moist kiss in the crook of her elbow.

"I can't love you, Adam. I won't. We're too different."

"Goodness, I hope so," he said with a soft chuckle as his lips nipped at her ear.

"That's not what I mean. Get serious." She reached up her hand to push his head away, but instead her fingers curled in the hair at the back of his neck and moved in lazy circles there.

"Oh, I am," he murmured as his lips caressed her throat. "I'm very serious." His head moved lower, taking first one nipple and then the other between his teeth, toying, tugging, inciting her body to riot.

Maggie closed her eyes and let the sensations sweep over her. Her hands reached up to explore the muscled strength of his back. Tension built within her as Adam's embraces traveled lower, and her body arched against his seeking tongue.

He murmured unintelligible things as his lips and tongue sought every crevice, every secret hollow, every inch of soft, yielding flesh on her body. The blood quickened in her veins as she rocked against him, fitting herself to his sensuous exploration.

"Adam," she whispered throatily. "Adam . . ." Her body took fire under the onslaught of his lips and tongue, writhing with wild abandon.

With the urgency of the first time gone, Adam took his leisure on his journey of love, lingering over her burning flesh until Maggie thought she would fly off the edge of the earth.

"Maggie . . ." he said softly as his lips left their

brand on her stomach. His mouth sought hers, melding them together in a scorching, searing kiss. Maggie opened to him, and once more they were forged together in an ancient bond.

With tantalizing slowness Adam moved against her, while outside their window, snow continued to blanket the earth in mounting fury. But they were oblivious to everything except the searing heat of love.

The pleasure built within them, creating its own storm. Maggie cried out as Adam carried her to the raging center of the storm and then brought her back out to the throbbing edges of its fury. Sweat glistened on their bodies as they hovered on the edges, drawing out the anticipation until it was strung between them as tight as a bowstring. Slowly they allowed the tumult to build again, until it exploded into a crashing, mind-shattering ecstasy.

Like a drowning man coming up for air, Adam leaned his dark head against her golden hair. "Maggie . . . Maggie. How can you deny our love?"

"Don't talk. Just hold me."

Maggie lay in his embrace, content to listen to the crackle of the fire and the combined thrumming of their hearts. She was afraid to move from her warm spot on the rug lest she leave behind all the magic she had found there. Her hand idly caressed Adam's shoulder. Her Adam. The man she had fought tooth and toenail. The man she had tried desperately to shove out of her heart.

"Are you cold, Maggie?" He lifted his head and looked at her.

She smiled a lazy cat's smile and shook her head.

"Well, I am."

"That's because you're on top and I'm on bottom."

"Some people have all the luck." He sat up and reached for the green shirt. Shrugging into it, he reached for the buttons and then grinned sheepishly as he realized they were lying scattered about the floor. "I don't suppose you sew?"

Maggie stretched and yawned. "I don't suppose you have any thread?"

"Never had occasion for it before. I don't make a habit of being a bodice-ripper."

Maggie laughed and sat up beside him. "Hey, that's my shirt."

"I guess we'll have to share." Adam pulled her onto his lap, crushed her against his chest, and wrapped the shirt around them both.

"It's a little small," she noted as she cuddled against his chest.

"But cozy, don't you think?"

"Hmmm." She took small, biting nips at his neck. "I hate to be mundane," she said between nibbles, "but do you have anything to eat in this cabin?"

"Just me."

"I mean anything else."

"I'm crushed. How can you prefer ordinary eggs to me?"

She leaned back in his arms and smiled up at him. "I don't suppose Jefferson Place would be interested in delivering an order of fried zucchini, do you?"

"Fifty miles? And in this snow?"

"Snow?" Maggie jumped up and ran to the window. "It's snowing," she wailed. "Why didn't you tell me it was snowing?" She whirled around to face Adam.

"I like you in the buff, Maggie. I think I'll keep you that way." Adam pulled on his jeans and fastened his belt buckle, then ran a hand through his tousled hair.

"How can you joke at a time like this? Where's the phone? I have to get out of here."

Adam walked up behind her and encircled her

with his arms. "I don't have a phone in the cabin. Anyway, I'm sure nothing is moving on the roads now, from the looks of this snow." He pulled her back up against his chest and propped his chin against her hair. "What's the matter, Maggie?"

"Don't you see? I can't stay here with you like this. It can never work for us. Our beliefs will tear us apart. You'll always be a hunter and I love animals, and that can never be reconciled."

"Shh." He swayed gently, rocking her in his arms. Taking her head in his hands, he turned her so that she was looking out the window. "Look how beautiful it is, Maggie. How many years has it been since you saw a snow like that in Mississippi?"

In silence they gazed together at the perfectly white world. The wind had stopped blowing, and the forest outside was a wonderland. As they watched, a pine bough too heavily laden tipped its load, and snow sifted to the ground like white powder.

"It's breathtaking." Maggie rested her head against Adam's shoulder as she reveled in the winter scene before them.

"It's like a gift, Maggie. A gift to us." Adam turned her in his arms so he could look into her eyes. "We'll be stranded here together until the snow and ice melt."

"No," she protested faintly.

His fingers traced her lips. "Yes." He bent over and placed a kiss on her forehead. "And while we're here, Maggie, we'll forget all about hunting and protesting and all the things that stand between us. It will be just the two of us and our love."

If Maggie had possessed a magic wand, she would have waved it over them, locking them forever in this time of love and beauty. She wanted to close out the world, to shut out reality, so it could just be the two of them, a man and a woman in love. She pressed against Adam, wrapping her arms around his middle. He seemed to understand her need for an interlude of fantasy, she thought.

"Just the two of us," she whispered.

"And . . ." he prompted. He wanted her to admit her love.

"I won't say it. It can't come true."

"Ever my stubborn tigress." He smiled adoringly at her.

"How about those eggs?" She grinned. "And some clothes."

"Party pooper," he chided her as he went to his closet and found her another of his shirts.

"That's what Martha Jo calls me," Maggie told him as she buttoned the blue-checked flannel shirt.

Adam reached out and stopped her hand two buttons down from the top. "I won't let you spoil all my fun."

"Are you a voyeur?" she teased.

"A shameless Peeping Tom where you're concerned." He took her hand and pulled her toward the kitchen area of the cabin. "How are you with eggs?"

"My eggs are on a par with my tea."

"Ugh. I'll do the cooking and you can do the washing up."

Maggie placed her hands on her hips and glared indignantly at him. "What's wrong with my tea?"

"Don't even ask, Maggie. It would take an Act of Congress to fix your tea." She could see Adam's shoulders shaking with laughter as he cracked eggs into a bowl.

"Then why were you so all-fired anxious to have a cup? 'I'm shivering in the cold, dying for the lack of a little hot tea,' " she said, mimicking the words he had used after the WI banquet.

"That's good, Maggie. Have you ever thought about a television career?" He whisked the eggs with a wire beater, his shoulders shaking with mirth.

"Why, you impostor! Posing as a tea lover just to get inside my house."

"I've found that subterfuge sometimes works with wary tigresses." His eyes twinkled with devilment as he crossed to the refrigerator. His voice was muffled as he called out to her. "How are you at chopping onions?"

"I don't chop onions. They make me cry."

"Then, you do the mushrooms; I'll do the onions." Adam tossed a box of fresh mushrooms over to her.

Maggie looked at them in astonishment. "Fresh mushrooms? In Tallahatchie River bottom?" She carried the mushrooms to the sink to wash them.

"I don't believe in roughing it when it comes to eating. I always bring groceries with me when I come to the cabin." His knife sliced through the onion and clicked against the cutting board.

Maggie selected a knife and joined him. "May I share your board?" Her nod indicated the cutting block.

"And my bed." He looked up and their eyes locked, fused by the passion that sizzled between them.

Maggie was the first to lower her eyes. Color suffused her cheeks at the import of his statement. She busied herself with the mushrooms, letting her hair sweep forward to cover her flaming face. Her knife slapped vigorously against the board as she thought of sharing that cherry four-poster with Adam.

Attempting to break the spell of sensuality that had settled over them, she spoke lightly. "I hope you're not a cover hog."

Adam leaned over and nipped at her ear. "Just a Maggie hog."

"What . . . what do you intend to do?" After what

they had shared on the rug beside the fire, there was no earthly reason for her to feel flustered. But she did. It had to be that cherry four-poster, she decided.

His eyebrows rose. "To do?"

"With the mushrooms, I mean." She glanced over toward the bed. It looked twice as big as it had before.

Adam chuckled. "I'm going to put them into this fantastic omelet, and then I'm going to sit at that table over there and have these eggs for my main course." He reached out and touched her cheek. "You will be dessert."

Maggie looked straight into his deep, blue eyes. How many times had she dreamed of herself in his arms and thought the dream impossible? How many times had she wanted to whisk him away for an idyll between perfumed sheets? And now he was right here in front of her, offering the romantic interlude of her dreams in his snowbound cabin.

Maggie's unaccustomed burst of shyness disappeared, and she lifted her chin. He was, after all, the man she had already loved so fiercely in the firelight. Her eyes sparkled when she spoke. "Then, Adam, I have a suggestion."

"What's that?"

"Let's hurry with the omelet."

"My sentiments exactly, Tigress."

They laughed and chatted together as the omelet browned in the pan. Outside, the pale sun dropped over the western horizon; inside, the cabin was suffused with the golden glow of firelight.

Adam lit a fat candle in a brass holder and brought it to the table. By its flickering flame they ate their omelets and delighted in their ease with each other.

"This is delicious, Adam. I didn't know how hungry I was." She took a big bite of the omelet. "Where did you learn to cook like this?"

"Cooking school."

"You're kidding."

"No, I'm not. After tiring of eating out all the time and suffering through my own inept attempts at preparing lonely bachelor meals, I enrolled in a course at Chez Cuisine."

"You must have graduated at the top of your class."

"I'm a man of many talents, Maggie."

"And I have an insatiable curiosity to discover them all."

"Then, Maggie, I have a suggestion." His eyes gleamed at her across the table.

"What?" she asked softly.

"Finish your omelet . . ." He let the sentence hang between them until the tension was a palpable thing. "In a hurry," he added as he moved around the table.

Lifting her golden tumble of hair, he planted a soft kiss on the back of her neck. Maggie turned in her chair and caught his face between her hands. "Adam?"

"Yes, Maggie?" The current between them sizzled and snapped.

"Do we have to do the dishes?"

"The dishes can wait." Taking her hands, he pulled her from the chair and into his arms. "They might have to wait a long time," he added as he nuzzled her neck.

Maggie entwined her arms around his waist as they moved together toward the bed. "Do you know what I think?" she said dreamily as the bed squeaked under their combined weight.

"Hmm?" he murmured as his hands worked to unfasten her buttons.

"I think you're full of wonderful suggestions," she said as they moved on to the dessert.

Ten

Maggie felt something tickling her nose. Sleepily she swatted with her hand and mumbled. The persistent something moved to tickle her ear. Groggily, she opened one eye.

"Good morning, sleepyhead." Adam was leaning on one elbow, smiling down into her face. With the quilt draped over his shoulders and his dark, tousled hair, he looked like a good-natured Indian chief. Except for his brilliant blue eyes.

Maggie's eyes snapped open, and she grinned like the cat that had stolen the cream. He looked too good to be true. She lifted one hand and pushed a dark strand of hair away from his forehead. "Good morning yourself," she said softly.

"Did anyone ever tell you how gorgeous you are in the morning?" His eyes swept hungrily over her honey-colored hair, spread across the pillow, and the soft down of her skin, gilded by the morning sun spilling through the window. "I could spend two hours just looking at you if I didn't have better things to do."

"Just name me one better thing to do," she teased.

"This." He bent down and kissed her eyelids. "And this." His lips brushed her cheek. "And this." He nuzzled her throat.

"That *is* better," she said as she wound her arms around his neck. "Much better," she said against his lips as they moved up to cover hers. And they had their dessert before breakfast.

Later, as she lay surfeited in his arms, she spoke of practical things. "Adam, what will I do for clothes?"

"I think clothes would hamper our style."

She rubbed her knuckles across his chin, reveling in the feel of his early-morning beard stubble. "Nothing would hamper your style." She settled herself comfortably against the warm cradle of his body. "When we get out of bed, we might go outside. Don't you think I'll need something to cover my body besides your shirt?"

"Don't worry about clothes. I plan to keep your body covered."

"You're incorrigible."

"You're incredible."

Behind her back, Maggie heard Adam yawn. She snuggled closer to him and drifted off to sleep.

They were both ravenously hungry when they finally got out of bed. Together they fixed a breakfast fit for loggers, and after they ate, they crowded into the shower stall for a very long bath.

"I've always wanted to bathe with a woman," Adam told her as the hot water swirled over their slick bodies.

"Just any woman?" Maggie asked pointedly. She slathered the soap lavishly onto his back, letting her hands drift in slow, sensuous circles across its smooth, muscled surface.

"Yes. Just any old woman."

Maggie swatted his backside with the wet washcloth.

"Particularly green-eyed blondes," Adam corrected himself quickly.

"That's better." Her voice became dreamy as she moved her hands over his soapy body and felt his rising need for her.

Slowly he turned in the hot, steamy bath and pressed against her softness. Their mouths met eagerly as the soap slipped from Maggie's fingers. The slipppery feel of their bodies only added fuel to the fire that was already raging out of control.

The water splashed around them unheeded as Adam's eyes became hooded and heavy. His tongue slipped into her open mouth with a desperate need, and she wound her legs around his hips as he lifted her to meet his powerful thrust.

His breathing was sharp and harsh in the close confines of the shower as they surged together in perfect rhythm, a rhythm made more beautiful because of their shared love.

And when at last the rhythm slowed and their breathing returned to normal, and Maggie rested her head on his slick shoulder, she marveled at the strength of her love for Adam. Was it possible that ever a woman had loved a man so? She sighed lustily against his shoulder. She thought not.

He released her hips, and her legs slid gently to the shower floor. His hand reached up to turn off the water. "And now, how about that walk in the snow, Maggie?" He took a fluffy towel and began rubbing her vigorously.

"You must be kidding. I was thinking of sitting moony-eyed in front of the fire all day long."

"Come on, Maggie. We're in the woods, and nature is calling." He wound the towel around her hips and leaned down to plant a moist kiss on one pouting breast.

"I thought it was lust."

He chuckled against her soft flesh. "I see I'm trapped with a hoyden."

"And a shameless one at that," she agreed as she kissed the top of his wet head.

After leaving their glorious bath behind, they managed to fit Maggie into a pair of Adam's jeans that settled rakishly about her hips. She buttoned one of his flannel shirts up to her neck and covered the whole stylish ensemble with a fleecy parka of his that fell halfway to her knees.

Adam looked at her scrubbed and shining face, devoid of makeup, and at the beautiful sparkle of her long-lashed cat's eyes. Planting a kiss atop her nose he ushered her out the door. "You look like a little girl playing grownup."

"That's not what you thought a moment ago." She pulled the hood of the parka over her hair as they stepped out into the white, frozen forest. Grabbing his hand, she pulled him through the snow. "Oh, Adam! Have you ever seen anything so beautiful!"

Their feet made deep tracks in the snow as they ran through the trees. Although the temperature was still in the teens, the sun shone down through the branches, glistening on the ice and snow, turning the forest into a thousand gleaming jewels.

Their breath made clouds in the air as they walked. The forest was silent except for the muffled scrunch of snow under their feet.

Suddenly Adam stopped, putting a restraining hand on Maggie's arm. "Look," he whispered. "Just ahead."

A white-tail deer was poised in the snow-covered thicket, his ears cocked and his shiny black nose sniffing the air. He was a young buck, with his rack just beginning to show evidence of another point.

They were downwind of the deer, so they stood still, undetected, as he arched his graceful neck and looked at the frozen world about him. Lifting a dainty hoof on a fragile-looking leg, he pawed the snow and then shook his head in annoyance as the unfamiliar powdery stuff sprayed around his nose.

Maggie and Adam had to cover their mouths to keep from laughing aloud at the deer's puzzlement. The movement of their arms alerted the young buck, and his head turned swiftly toward them in alarm. For an instant his soulful brown eyes held them, and then he leaped into the thicket. Maggie and Adam saw a flash of white, the underside of the deer's tail, as he disappeared into the forest.

With Adam's hand still on Maggie's arm, they stood still, afraid to look at each other, knowing that the buck had brought their differences to the surface.

"I don't see how you could . . ."

"Now I see why . . ."

They both spoke at once. Adam looked down at Maggie. "I know what you were thinking, Maggie."

Their gaze held for a moment before Maggie turned away. Looking off into the forest, she spoke softly. "It's always there between us, isn't it?"

Adam pulled her into his arms and crushed her against his chest. "Don't say it, Maggie. I won't let it be between us. I love you."

She pressed her cheeks against the rough wool of his jacket and dug her fingers into his coat sleeves. "Oh, Adam! Why?"

And he understood her anguished cry, her need to know how he could hunt an animal so beautiful. "There's a primitive challenge in the hunt, a pitting of man against beast. It's not the thrill of the kill, Maggie. That is anticlimactic. There is a moment just before the trigger is pulled when man has triumphed over nature, when he has fulfilled that ancient urge to embroil himself in conflict and to prevail. Without that struggle, man is a double-edged sword hacking away at crabgrass."

He felt her shudder against him, and his arm tightened around her. "But hunting is more than that, Maggie. A true sportsman never kills over the limit and always uses his game for food. He is also one of the greatest animal conservationists in the country."

"No," she protested against his coat. "It's not true."

"Yes. The money collected from hunting and fishing licenses is used to pay for conservation efforts and for the salaries of game wardens whose job it is to protect the animals."

"They wouldn't need protection if it weren't for the hunters."

"Do you know what would happen if there were no hunting?"

Her head snapped up. "Of course. The animals would live."

"That's simplistic, Maggie. They would overpopulate until their feeding grounds could no longer support them, and then they would die of starvation and disease."

"That's survival of the fittest, Adam. Nature's way."

"But without hunters and the laws we made to protect game animals, they would be slaughtered by the hundreds, like the buffalo, until there were no more left."

What he said made sense, but she couldn't adjust emotionally to the killing. "Didn't you see his graceful neck and the shiny smoothness of his coat? Hunting is not just the snuffing out of life; it's the destruction of beauty."

"I saw, Maggie." His voice was quiet. "And I appreciate that beauty." He cupped her cheeks with his hands and looked into her face. They hardly breathed as they looked at each other. The air sizzled with undercurrents. Doubts and uncertainties swirled between them and disappeared, submerged by the powerful current of sexual awareness that left them breathless.

"You have a choice, Maggie." His deep voice was the only sound in the silent forest.

A cold hand clutched at her heart. She wasn't ready to choose. How could she ever choose between this man she adored and the animals she loved? She swallowed a lump in her throat and looked at Adam with wide green eyes. "What?" Her voice was barely a whisper.

Suddenly he grinned. Maggie could feel the sunshine of his smile lighting up the entire Tallahatchie River bottom. "Kiss me and create a little body heat or stand there and freeze."

She reached her arms around his broad shoulders and lifted her mouth to his. As their lips met and the familiar fire spread through her, turning her bones to hot maple syrup, Maggie was fleetingly aware of her cause, fading to a mere shadow in the corners of her mind.

"I wonder what it would be like to make love in the snow?" Adam murmured as he devoured her lips.

"Don't . . . you . . . dare," she said between kisses. "We'd . . . freeze."

A heavy pine bough above them drooped and deposited its load of snow on Maggie's head. "Brr! That's cold." She broke the kiss and shook her head, sending snow flying.

Adam laughed. "You look like a cocker spaniel."

"Oh, I do, do I?" Devilment danced in Maggie's eyes as she bent down and carefully lobbed a fistful of snow into Adam's face. "Let's see how you look."

The fight was on. Like two high-spirited children, they scooped up the snow, packed it into balls, and sailed them through the air at each other. Maggie proved to have the most lethal aim, and Adam found himself dodging more than he threw.

"Truce, Maggie!" he yelled as one of her well-aimed snowballs found its mark on his nose.

"You say that just because you're losing." Gleefully she lobbed two at once, which found their mark on his broad chest.

"Maggie!" Adam roared as he charged. He came bounding across the snow toward her like an avenging bear.

Her feet flew across the snow as she ran lithely before him. She felt carefree and giddy and wonderfully alive. Ducking behind a cottonwood tree she waited, breathless, for Adam to find her. Her cold, wet hand clutched her throat, and her green eyes sparkled like gems as she leaned against the tree trunk.

The seconds ticked by, and there was no sound in the forest except her own ragged breathing. The seconds stretched out, and anticipation quivered in Maggie as if a phantom hand had plucked the bowstrings of her heart.

Cautiously she stuck her head around the tree trunk. "Adam?"

Splat! "Got you!" he yelled as the snowball caught her squarely in the face.

"Oh, you . . ." She wiped the cold, powdery flakes from her face with both hands.

"You what?" Adam's arms encircled her waist as he pulled her down into the snow.

"Sneaky," she sputtered as she lay atop him.

He caught her face between his hands and brought it close, so that their noses touched. With careful precision, his tongue outlined her icy lips, licking away the moist snow.

"Hmm, good. And what else?"

"Underhanded," she murmured against his

chilled skin as she peppered small kisses all over his face.

"How about hungry?" He rolled her over, so that her golden hair was spread out upon the snow. One of his legs was thrown across her hips, molding her to him so that even through their thick clothes she could feel the glorious outline of his desire.

"How can you be hungry? We just ate." Her warm breath fanned against his cheek as her fingers lovingly traced his jaw.

"For you." His mouth descended swiftly, and he very thoroughly communicated just how hungry he was. Snowball fights and wild animals and forty-four-magnum guns and bright silver trumpets melted and dissolved into a puddle of nothingness before the fierce onslaught of his lips.

The cold snow and the damp frozen ground could have been softest eiderdown for all Maggie knew as she clung to Adam, mindlessly answering his kiss. They rolled together, legs entangled, as they sought relief from the fire that enveloped them.

Maggie was only dimly aware of being scooped into his arms and carried to the cabin. His footsteps were muffled by the snow, and his progress was hampered as he stopped at intervals to press his burning lips to hers.

Her fingers were already working on the buttons of his shirt when Adam kicked the cabin door shut behind them. Clothing made an untidy trail across the floor as they made their heady progress toward the fire. The shaggy fingers of the rug caressed Maggie's bare back as she welcomed Adam into her soft, secret warmth.

"I love you, Maggie," he whispered hoarsely into her ear, and then the world was blotted out.

Much later, she lay sprawled across Adam's

chest like a contented cat as her fingers idly played in the crisp dark hair on his chest.

"Do you know what I think?" she asked dreamily.

"Hmm?" Adam was content to lie on the rug with Maggie in his arms and the fire warming his backside.

Maggie looked at their strewn, snow-soaked clothes. "I think if we continue this—" her lips curved into a satisfied smile, "cavorting, we'll not have a single thread left to wear."

"Is that what you call this? Cavorting?"

"Umm . . . awe-inspiring sex."

"I call it love." His vivid blue eyes bored into hers, belying the lightness of his voice.

Maggie turned her face to the fire to avoid his eyes. She couldn't say the words. If she said, "I love you, Adam," she was committed and there would be no turning back. The blaze leaped and crackled in the fireplace, and sparks shot out from the fire, falling harmlessly on the brick apron and changing to black, dying embers. That was what she would be without Adam, she thought, a lifeless lump. A dead ember. Maggie sighed lustily and wished they could stay trapped forever in the woods, shut off from the world, wrapped in the soft cocoon of their love.

"Do you know what this occasion calls for?" Adam stood and swatted Maggie lightly on her naked hip. Ever aware of her moods, he sought to dispel the sadness he felt creeping over her. He seemed instinctively to know when she felt the heavy weight of their differences descend between them. "Taffy."

"Taffy?" She looked up in amazement. "What's the occasion, and whatever brought taffy to your mind?" She stood up and slipped her arms into the flannel shirt.

"The occasion is us together in the snow, and

cooking a batch of taffy is the way my grandmother celebrates big events."

She watched the way his slim hips moved in the tight-fitting jeans as he walked, shirtless, across to the kitchen. With all the efficiency of a man who knows what he is doing, Adam began to rattle pots and pans.

She followed, her bare feet whispering on the wooden floor, and leaned against the cabinet. "Don't tell me you know how to make taffy."

"I won't tell you. I'll show you." Adam whistled as he measured sugar and corn syrup and butter into a large aluminum-lined copper pot.

"I suppose you learned that at cooking school."

"Nope." He took a wooden spoon and stirred the sugary mixture. "Grandmother Trent taught me. She is quite a lady. When I was a child, I spent every Saturday night at her house. 'Now, Adam,' she'd say, 'since I don't have any granddaughters and Heaven knows! it doesn't look like Paul and Martha are going to give me any, I'm going to teach you how to make taffy.' And then she'd set me on a tall kitchen stool and let me stir."

Maggie listened with fascination. Adam Trent had a grandmother. How wonderful! She loved families. All she'd had were Dad and Jim. She wanted her children to know the love of aunts and uncles and grandpas and great-grandmothers. Adam had a grandmother! She beamed at him.

"You said 'is.' That means she's still living?" She leaned forward, her eyes shining and her honey-and-wheat hair tumbling across her shoulders.

"Yes. On Highland Circle, in Tupelo. She lives with two cats—the parents of Beauregard—a sassy myna bird, and a bossy housekeeper named Elijah Jane."

"Elijah?"

"Cross my heart and hope to die. She said her pappy swore to name his first child after his favorite biblical character and she had the good fotune to be born first." The taffy bubbled in the pan as they talked, permeating the cabin with a lip-smackingly sweet, buttery smell.

"The *good* fortune?"

"That's what she said."

"Oh, I can't wait to meet them." Maggie clapped her hands in glee, forgetting her stubborn refusal to acknowledge a future for them. "I've always dreamed of having lots of kids and going to family reunions with great-grandmas and doting aunts and adoring uncles and lots of pets and Elijah Janes."

"That's what our children will have, Maggie."

Our children? Our children! Maggie clapped her hands over her mouth. What had she said? "Oh, I didn't mean . . . I just meant . . ." Her thoughts ran squirrellike around the cage of her mind, trying to find an escape. There was none. "How's the taffy coming?" she asked faintly.

Very carefully Adam took the pot off the stove, trying hard to keep a straight face. An occasional twitch at the corners of his mouth betrayed his mirth. "About ready for pulling."

It was quiet in the cabin except for the splat of wooden spoon against cooling taffy. Maggie watched the muscles ripple in Adam's smooth back as he beat the mouth-watering mixture. Our children, our children, her heart sang, while doubt reared its ugly head in the dark corners of her mind. Oh, how could she ever leave Adam? she wondered, anguished at the thought.

"Maggie?"

More than anything in the world she wanted to have his children. She wanted to go to sleep at night and wake up in the morning in his arms. Everything would have been perfect—except for the animals.

"Maggie?"

158 • PEGGY WEBB

She snapped to attention. Adam was smiling at her across a smooth, cream-colored mass of candy. "Grab that end and pull."

Gingerly she took a sticky mass in her hands. "Now what?"

"Pull, Maggie. It won't bite." Adam laughed at the way she stepped cautiously backward, holding the taffy stiffly in front of her. "Haven't you ever made taffy?"

"No. There was only Dad, Jim, and me. I had one grandparent living when I was born—Papa Merriweather—but he died while I was still too young to remember much about him. I missed all the family activities most kids have."

"So you filled your life with animals?"

"Yes." She gave the taffy a sharp pull. No wonder Adam was the youngest bank president Mutual had ever had, she thought. He understood people. "Why are we doing this, Adam?" She gave the string of sticky taffy a jiggle.

"So it will be smooth and chewy. Wait and see." Adam walked toward Maggie, doubling back the long string of candy so they could start afresh with the pulling. His hands covered hers as he put the ends of the taffy together. "Making taffy with my grandmother was never like this!" He raised one eyebrow and leered at her cleavage, visible above the third button of her shirt.

He looked so adorable standing there, she thought suddenly, and he was so close it would be a shame not to hug him. Maggie's arms wound around his neck.

"Maggie! The taffy!"

It was too late. The taffy was draped around his neck, hanging in sticky strings down his bare chest.

Maggie dissolved into laughter. The undersides of her arms were stickily attached to Adam's neck and the hairs on his chest. "Oh—" she gasped, taking great gulps of air to try and stop laughing, "I think we're stuck."

"Probably permanently," he agreed amiably as he bent to taste her lips.

"Adam, the taffy!" Her lips were muffled against his.

"Yeah. There are things Grandmother Trent didn't tell me about the taffy." He lifted one of her arms and began to leisurely nibble away the bits of candy clinging there.

Maggie tasted a string of candy on the side of his neck. "You were right. This *is* smooth . . ." Her tongue made a hot little circle against his skin. ". . . and chewy." She playfully nipped his neck.

"Marry me, Maggie." He said it just like that, right in the middle of the taffy.

"What did you say?"

"I said, 'Marry me, Maggie.' " He casually licked a sticky glob of candy from one of her fingers.

Her heart thumped so loudly in her chest, she was sure it could be heard clear to Belden. There it was. The question she had been afraid he would ask and terrified that he wouldn't. And she wasn't ready to give him an answer. She wasn't even sure there was an answer. "Be sensible, Adam."

"Sensible?" The laughter rumbled deep in his chest as it heaved stickily against her shirt. "The world's all-time master of nonsense and deviltry wants me to be sensible? The tigress with the horn tells me to be sensible!"

"Well, somebody has to. You know I can't marry you."

"Why not?"

"You know damn well. Our differences would destroy us."

"Love allows differences, Maggie. Marry me."

"Our problem is more than just differences. It's a volcano under us ready to erupt."

"I'm partial to volcanoes."

"And can you imagine me at a bankers' meeting? The tigress with the horn?"

"I love tigresses." He kissed the tip of her nose. "And horns." He kissed her eyelashes. "Marry me."

"You're out of your mind." She tried to pull away from him and found herself bound by the taffy.

"Thank goodness for taffy." Adam squeezed her close, nuzzling her hair with his lips. "Say yes, Maggie."

"No, Adam." Her heart thundered in her chest. "I can never marry you."

"I'll make you change your mind."

Eleven

Maggie was wide awake. She had no idea what time it was. One pale moonbeam penetrated the blackness of the room, and outside, a screech owl was sending its eerie call through the night.

In spite of the warmth of the covers, Maggie shivered. A crushing sense of loss pressed against her heart, and she felt desolate. Carefully she lifted Adam's arm from her chest and climbed out of bed. The chill air of the cabin struck her naked body, and she reached for the flannel shirt on the chair beside the bed.

Her eyes became accustomed to the darkness, and, as she buttoned the shirt, she looked at the form on the bed. Adam was sleeping on his back, with one arm flung across her side of the bed and the covers pushed down from his chest. His left leg was sticking out from under the quilt, and his dark hair was tousled across his forehead. In sleep his face looked boyish and relaxed and completely vulnerable.

Maggie tiptoed around the bed and carefully pulled the covers back over his leg and up across his chest. Her hands lingered as she softly smoothed the quilt around him. Then she stiffened and left the bed.

The dying embers of last night's fire provided small comfort against the cold as Maggie walked to the window. Pressing her forehead against the icy pane, she looked out into the dark woods. The owl's cry echoed through the night. It was a lonesome, mournful cry, sadly appropriate for the moment.

Tears slid down Maggie's cheek and merged with the moisture on the windowpanes. Why couldn't life be simple? she wondered sadly. Why couldn't she have said "yes" that afternoon in the middle of the taffy? She loved Adam so fiercely that it made her weak just to think about it. But it was an impossible love. They might as well be on two separate continents, their differences were so great.

Maggie turned from the dark window and moved toward the fireplace. She sat on the hearth rug, pulling her knees up and resting her chin on them. The faint glow of the embers tinted the tears that still rained down her face, washing her skin with red-gold. She and Adam were both strong-willed people. If she married him, she was sure their differences would fester under the surface until they finally eroded the marriage and destroyed them both. And she couldn't let that happen. Marriage for her was a lifetime commitment, not just a short-term agreement. She couldn't commit herself to Adam knowing that the future was so shaky and uncertain. She couldn't marry the man she loved, knowing that the love would eventually destroy him.

She wiped her shirt sleeve across her face, drying the tears that glistened there. Outside, the owl's cry sounded fainter as the night bird moved deeper into the forest. Maggie hugged her lonesomeness around her and sat very still, listening. The owl's cry was a death knell, mingling with the sound of her own broken heart, a haunted dirge for the death of a marriage that could never be.

"Maggie?" The quiet voice came from behind her.

She turned her head to see Adam standing a few feet away, watching her intently. The anguish on her face sent him a silent message, and his response was immediate.

Swiftly he was beside her, cradling her in his arms. With his lips on her hair, he murmured, "Maggie, Maggie, love. What's wrong?"

"Nothing," she whispered, burying her face in his shoulder.

He rocked her gently in his arms, not saying a word, giving her time to share her anguish with him.

"Everything." She gulped back the tears that were collecting in her throat. Gripping his shoulders with both hands, she looked up into his face. "It's us, Adam. We're impossible." Her look asked him to deny the statement, begged him to prove her wrong.

"No," he said, firmly. "I love you, Maggie, and I know we can make it work."

"How?" Her green eyes challenged him in the dim light of the room. "Just tell me how."

She hardly breathed as she looked up at him for an answer. The waiting stillness filled the room, hanging in the air and smothering the two people who sat before the fire in a blanket of anticipation.

"Maggie, don't deny us before we have a chance." Adam's breath warmed the skin behind her ear as his harsh whisper broke the silence.

Maggie's hands moved to cup his face, bringing it close, so that she could capture his lips. "Oh, Adam! I need you, Adam. I need you to comfort me

. . . now." Her last words were muffled by the desperate joining of their lips. As the first faint rays of dawn crept across the windowsill and rose-tinted the light in the cabin, Adam and Maggie tried to deny their differences with impassioned lovemaking.

Later they stood at the window and watched the rising sun tint the forest with its changing rainbow of colors. Deep rose became a pale pink that finally gave way to brilliant gold.

Maggie rested her head against Adam's shoulder and watched nature's gorgeous color show. "The sun's up."

"Yes." His arms tightened around her as if the approaching sun might snatch her away.

"It's going to be a sunny day, Adam."

They both knew what that meant. The sun would melt all the snow, and they would no longer have an excuse for staying in their wonderful forest hideaway.

She turned in his arms, her face already filled with the pain of her leaving. "Let's build a snowman." Her words were almost a plea, a desperate attempt to continue the fantasy that she and Adam could live happily ever after in his snowbound cabin, shut away from proper bank meetings and improper belly-dancing, protected from hunters' guns and horn-tooting causes.

"Before breakfast?" His smile was crooked as he gazed lovingly down at her.

Maggie arched her neck and gave him a Madonna smile, a smile that said she knew all the secrets of the world . . . except the one she needed most—how they could be together. "I find 'before breakfast' a good time for many activities."

"So I've noticed."

"Are you complaining?"

"Gloating."

"You just saved yourself a severe drubbing in the

snow." She broke away from his arms and raced to the bedside chair to grab her borrowed jeans. "Last one outside is a rotten egg."

She quickly fastened the jeans around her hips and bolted for the door a full minute before Adam. The sharp coolness of the morning air and the brilliance of the snow in the sun took her breath away. She stood on the porch, savoring the beauty, and then she jumped down the steps and hastily formed a snowball.

With feigned innocence she hid the snowball behind her back and waited for Adam. He bounded down the steps and scooped her up in his arms.

"Does the rotten egg get a kiss?" His blue eyes sparkled.

"No," she said archly.

"Well, in that case"—he dumped her unceremoniously onto the snow—"let's make a snowman." Whistling nonchalantly, he turned his back to her and began rolling snow for the body.

"Adam."

He looked back over his shoulder, and she lobbed the snowball right into his face. "Catch," she yelled gleefully.

By the time they had finished the lopsided snowman and argued heatedly over who'd won the snowball fight, the sun was high in the sky, and ice was melting off the trees.

Together they prepared a huge meal that he called breakfast and she called lunch. Outside they could hear water dripping off the eaves as the cover of snow and ice succumbed to the bright sun. Gaiety ran high as they devoured their food and tried not to think about tomorrow.

They spent the afternoon trekking through the forest, arm in arm, discovering the beauty of the woods as if it existed only for them. Their pleasure in their walk was tinged with sadness, and their hike was frequently interrupted by desperate embraces.

Once, when they neared the edge of the Tallahatchie River, Adam attempted to break through the wall of silence that Maggie had built around the subject of marriage.

"Marry me, Maggie. We can work things out."

"No." She looked at the muddy river meandering through the trees, its course already charted. If only she could be like the river! she wished silently. But she was only human, and she had to chart her own course. Right or wrong, she believed that she couldn't chart her course with Adam's. Two raging currents together would be devastating. "I just can't."

He caught her fiercely to his chest. "Stubborn Maggie." His palms held her face and his thumbs gently traced her lips. "I'm not going to give up, you know."

"Let it go, Adam. We've had our time together. We'll have our memories." How could she make such an asinine statement, when her heart was breaking in two? she thought bitterly. She tried to put on a brave smile so Adam wouldn't see the depth of her struggle.

"Damn." He released her and scowled at the river. Suddenly he turned, and practically dragged her all the way back to the cabin. By the time he had kicked the door shut behind them, they were both shedding their clothes.

The late-day sun caressed their intertwined bodies as it poured through the west window of the cabin. Maggie raised herself onto one elbow and looked down into Adam's face. Her hair fell across one side of her face and made a silken curtain on Adam's shoulder.

"Remember when you swore to tame me?" With her free hand she traced the outline of his lips.

"Um-hmm."

"I think you just did."

"I'm going to remind you of that fifty years from now." His voice was light and teasing, but his eyes studied Maggie keenly.

Fifty years from now meant the two of them together. But it was an impossible dream, Maggie reminded herself. Why couldn't Adam see that? Maggie climbed out of the cherry four-poster, certain that nothing he could say could change her mind.

A light shudder ran through her as she donned Adam's flannel shirt. This would be their last evening together, and both of them knew it. The sun had rapidly melted the snow and ice. By tomorrow morning the roads would be passable.

With her back still to Adam, Maggie let her hands linger on the soft flannel as she fastened the buttons. "I'll miss your shirts."

There was no reply from the bed. She buttoned the top button. And I'll miss you, she thought. Most of all, I'll miss you. "Are you hungry?" Still no reply. "I thought we could pop some corn by the fire. You do have a long-handled popper, don't you?" She was chattering to cover the issue that haunted them both. "Do you know that in all the time we've been here we haven't popped any corn by the fire? I don't even know if you like yours with butter."

She felt rather than saw Adam as he passed quietly by her on the way to the refrigerator. The firelight bronzed his bare back as he rummaged around. He emerged holding two steaks in his hands. "Man cannot live by love alone," he quipped.

Relieved that he had chosen not to pursue the

subject of marriage, Maggie smiled. "I'd watch out for stray thunderbolts if I were you," she teased.

Their teasing set the tone for the rest of the evening. When, at last, the moon was riding high in the sky and the plaintive call of the owl sounded in the forest, Maggie and Adam snuggled contentedly in the four-poster, with nothing between them except their love.

"You really are determined to go?" Adam leaned against the mantel and studied Maggie.

"I thought I had already made myself clear." She touched the side of Adam's face with her fingertips, running them across the stubble of his beard. "Oh, Adam, don't look at me like that."

"How?"

"That look you have." It was both possessive and predatory, she thought, the look of a man deeply in love, the look of a man determined not to be thwarted. "I won't change my mind."

"Neither will I."

"Then, I guess it's a stalemate."

"Stalemates can be broken." The words were spoken solemnly, almost like a promise.

Maggie's green eyes widened and changed as she looked at him. There was nothing quite like the power of a determined man in love, she decided sadly. Maggie sent a prayer winging upward that she would be able to get into her truck and turn the key, that she would be able to leave Adam Trent standing in the woods with his impossible dream. But most of all, she prayed that she could get around the bend in the road before she cried.

"I'm ready to go." Her voice trembled when she spoke. She watched Adam's face to see if he noticed. He did. His hands reached out to draw her to him.

"Maggie. My wild, willful Maggie." His lips

devoured hers, pleading, demanding that she change her mind. When at last he lifted his head, his eyes were the dark blue of storm clouds. "You're my obsession, Maggie. I'll never let you go."

"You have no choice." Maggie broke away from him and walked toward the door. "Coming?"

Silently they slogged over the slushy ground to her parked truck. Maggie looked wistfully around the forest and fought back the tears. Nothing would ever be the same for her again.

She watched as Adam laid pine boughs under the wheels of her truck and backed it out of the mud. She felt desolate and forlorn, but she knew that she was right. She loved Adam too much to marry him and let their differences destroy them.

Adam jumped down from the cab. His muddy jacket, which had sat in her truck for three days, was slung across his arm, and there was a tight line around his mouth. Suddenly, his arm snaked out and pulled her into his embrace, crushing her fiercely to his chest. "Stay."

"No." Staying would just be postponing the inevitable, Maggie reminded herself. A clean break was best. She clung to him a heartbreaking instant longer, and then she gently pushed herself out of his arms. "Good-bye, Adam." Lifting her chin high, she marched bravely to her waiting truck.

The cold engine, which had been unused for three days, sputtered and backfired. "Come on," she begged. "Don't fail me now." It coughed to life, and Maggie backed out of the forest.

Catching her trembling lower lip between her teeth, she watched Adam in the rearview mirror. He looked as rugged and solid as one of the great trees in the forest—and just as impassive. Only his eyes showed his pain. Maggie watched him until she rounded a bend in the road and he was out of sight.

And then the dam burst. The tears started as a

small trickle and gained momentum, until they were a river flooding her face. By the time she reached New Albany, she was crying so hard she had to pull over. "Damn." She beat her fists on the steering wheel. "Dammit all. Why does it have to be so hard?"

A prowl car pulled up beside her, and a highway patrolman tapped on her window. "Are you all right, ma'am?"

She wiped her eyes with her fists and smiled tremulously at him through her tears. "Yes. I'm just . . . just . . . Oh, Adam!" The tears started anew.

"I don't know who the hell Adam is, but he needs his butt whipped for making a pretty little thing like you cry." The patrolman's face was puckered up with concern. He thrust a large, hairy hand into his trouser pocket. "Here. Take this."

She took the handkerchief he offered and blew her nose. "Thank you. I didn't have one."

"You can keep it, ma'am." He shoved his hat back on his gray hair and scratched his head. "Are you going to be all right now?"

Her lips quivered as she smiled. "Yes. Thank you."

"Well, you drive safe, now, you hear? And call somebody when you get home. It's not good to be alone when you're down in the dumps like that."

"I will," she promised. She pulled the pickup onto the road, and the fatherly patrolman lifted his hand in farewell. She gave him a small wave and headed home.

Maggie's dogs were ecstatic when she stepped out of her truck. They barked joyously and wagged their tails so hard she thought they would fall into a heap on the carport floor. Bending over, she hugged them. "Did you miss me?"

They licked her hands and face. Silly girl, they seemed to be saying, of course they had missed her. They followed her into the house and watched with interest as she went straight to the cabinet to get their food. Taking care of her pets' needs allowed Maggie to push Adam into a dark corner of her mind.

She chattered away to her pets, postponing the moment when she would have to face her problem. "I can tell that your feeder didn't run out. And I see you've been hogging the food, as usual, Muffin."

The lively animals soon lost interest in the lavish attentions of their mistress and wandered off to more exciting pursuits. Maggie was left to face her heartbreak in her empty house.

Her blue Tiffany goblet winked at her from the kitchen windowsill, and she was reminded of how Adam's eyes had looked in the firelight of the cabin. Biting the inside of her cheek, she took the goblet and thrust it to the back of a cabinet. She set her teapot on to boil, the simple routine providing a brief moment of sanity in the turmoil that threatened to swamp her. Oh, Lord, she wondered, had she been right? She loved Adam so much! Already the doubts were beginning to assail her. If she had stayed, could they somehow have worked out their differences?

She paced restlessly as she waited for the water to boil. Her boots echoed hollowly in the empty house, empty of everything except memories. The bufflehead ducks above her mantel seemed to fill her den. She flew back to the kitchen as if demons were pursuing her.

Snatching up the kitchen phone, she dialed her father. "Please be back." The phone rang five times, and she had almost given up when she heard her father's voice. "Dad, is that you?" She strained across the distance that separated them, seeking her father's loving reassurance and support.

"Of course it is, darlin'. Who did you expect?"

"I wasn't sure you'd be back from your cruise. Did you have fun?" Her voice broke on the last word. Fun was Adam in the snow. Adam in front of the fire. Adam covered with taffy.

"Maggie, are you all right? You sound peculiar."

"I'm okay. I just wanted to see how . . . oh, Dad," she wailed. "I'm in love with Adam Trent." She sniffed loudly into the receiver, trying to hold back the tears.

"Well, darlin', you sound like it's a catastrophe. Has he done something to hurt you?"

"He's asked me to marry him."

"Oh, I see." There was silence at her father's end of the line as he mulled over the situation. He knew very well that his daughter had opposed Adam bitterly over the past weeks. He also knew her stubborn nature and her loyalty and devotion to her causes. The struggle had to be costing her dearly. He longed to reach out and ease her pain, to share the wisdom born of experience and make her choice for her, but he knew that only Maggie could make that choice. "Follow your heart, Maggie." He spoke the words softly, almost like a benediction.

"My heart is divided, Dad. I don't know where it will lead me."

"You'll find out, darlin'. Just give yourself some time."

Time. That was exactly what she needed. Time away from home, where even the teapot on the stove spoke eloquently of Adam. Its demanding whistle sounded from the kitchen.

"I think I'll leave home for a few days, Dad. Go up to Gatlinburg and rent a ski chalet."

"That's a good idea, Maggie. Do you need any money? I didn't leave everything I'd saved down in Mexico."

"Thanks, Dad, but I think I'm okay. I'll see you in a few days."

"All right, darlin'. I'll tell Jim where you're going. And Maggie, a little prayer wouldn't hurt."

"I know. 'Bye, Dad." She cradled the receiver gently. Talking with her father always made Maggie feel better. She had been desolate when she left Adam. She had believed that their love was impossible, their problems insurmountable. But now she wasn't sure. Her father's advice had offered a small glimmer of hope.

Maggie drank her cup of tea and then walked to the bedroom to pack her bags. Tomorrow she would drive to Gatlinburg.

She had lost something very precious. Something that she wanted desperately to find. Maggie sat straight up in bed. "Adam!" Her hand reached out and clutched an empty pillow.

Fully awake now, Maggie hugged the pillow to her chest in the darkness of her bedroom at the ski chalet. She had been dreaming, and in that half-conscious state, the truth had shown itself to her with perfect clarity. That "something precious" was Adam, and she couldn't stand to lose him.

Impatient with the dark, impatient with herself, and impatient even with Adam, she climbed out of bed and felt her way through the dark to the kitchen. Her fingers fumbled against the wall until she found the light switch. Blinking at the sudden blaze of light, Maggie adjusted her sleep-filled eyes and squinted at the clock. Five o'clock. The silent hour of early birds, early risers, and . . . hunters.

Maggie slumped down in a chair beside the table and rested her head on her crossed arms. There it was again. Just as real and as scary as ever. In spite of her love for Adam, could she ever adjust to his hunting? Could she learn to live with it? She was no closer to the answer than she had been two days ago, when she came to the ski chalet.

174 • PEGGY WEBB

Morosely Maggie rose from her chair and walked to the refrigerator. She never could think on an empty stomach. As she put the bacon on to fry, her mind was filled with Adam, with the love they had shared in the Tallahatchie River bottom cabin, and with the aching loneliness she had felt these last two days without him. There *had* to be a way, she thought desperately.

Maggie buttered two pieces of toast and popped them onto her plate with the bacon and eggs. Now that her mind was actively searching for a solution rather than denying any possibility of a future for them, she was ravenous.

Her fork clinked against the plate as she lifted the first piece of bacon to her mouth. Suddenly she sat dead still, the fork poised in the air. That was it! Of course, that was it! She burst out laughing. She laughed so hard that tears rolled down her cheek, tears of joy.

"Thank the Lord for bacon," she announced to the empty room. The truth had been there all along; she had just been too stubborn to see it. Bacon started out as pigs, little animals with pink, pointy ears and squiggly tails. That was what Adam had tried to explain: true sportsmen used the game they killed for food. And how was that different from steak or bacon or lamb chops?

She finished her breakfast with relish. When it was viewed in that light, she could not only tolerate Adam's hunting, she could even understand it. She sipped her tea and looked out the window to the mountains, growing pink with the first glow of dawn.

With the thorniest question of all solved, the rest came easy for Maggie. She wanted to make a home for Adam. She wanted picnics and family dinners and long, leisurely evenings by the fire with the man she loved. And she wanted children. Lots of them. She would not have as much time for her causes. Martha Jo could take over as president of FOA, and Maggie would work with them when she had time. There probably were more conventional and perhaps even better ways of achieving their goals. She'd think about that later. Right now, Adam was the only cause she had on her mind.

By the time Maggie had dressed in a fuzzy green jogging suit that matched her eyes, the sun was gilding the tops of the mountains with bright gold. She zipped into town, made her purchases, and zoomed back to the chalet, humming the entire time.

She spread a piece of heavy poster board on the floor. Getting down on her hands and knees, she worked with a black magic marker, grinning broadly as her hand raced across the poster. She laughed aloud as the bold black letters took shape. She would go straight to his bank with her sign. She'd mount the check-writing table again and this time announce to the whole world that she loved Adam Trent.

She sat back on her heels and viewed the finished work. Not bad, considering that the entire time she had been working on it she had thought of nothing except being in Adam's arms.

A raucous blaring outside her door brought her to her feet. There it was again! A wobbly, brassy sound that put Maggie in mind of one of Jim's sick cows bellowing.

Someone pounded loudly on her door. "Maggie! Open up and let me in."

Adam! Her bare feet flew across the tiled floor. She flung open the door and catapulted herself into his arms. "Oh, Adam. Oh, Lord, I'm glad to see you." She showered kisses on his surprised face. "I love you, Adam Trent."

"Say that again." His eyes drank in her face, savoring every last detail.

"I'm glad to see you," she teased.

"No, Tigress. The other."

"I do love you, Adam Trent. I really do!"

He carried her across the threshold and set her on her feet. His eyes roamed up and down her body as if he could never get his fill of looking. "If you hadn't said that, I was going to drag you off to the altar anyhow."

"And ruin your reputation as a staid old bank president?"

"I'm afraid my reputation is ruined anyway." He grinned sheepishly as he held up his right hand. A shiny new silver trumpet was clutched in his fingers.

"Is that what I heard?" Maggie burst into laughter. "Oh, Adam, you're terrible on the trumpet. Have you ever considered the piccolo?"

"The man at the music store suggested I buy a set of drums after he made me toot this damned horn. He said I didn't have the lips for playing brass. I told him he wouldn't have any teeth if he didn't just wrap up the damned horn and be quick about it."

Maggie took the silver trumpet from his hands and wrapped her arms around his neck. "I know what you *do* have lips for, Adam Trent. Come here." And she showed him.

When she came up for air she was full of questions. "How did you find me and why did you come and why the silver trumpet?"

"Your dad told me after I calmed down and convinced him I was not a crazed maniac. Oh, Lord, Maggie. I was like a grizzly bear with a toothache after you left me." He crushed her fiercely to his chest. "The silver trumpet is my sign to you. I'm giving it all up. The guns, the hunting, everything. You're all I want, Maggie."

His lips swooped down to claim hers, and her feeble "no" was smothered. His hands roamed across her bare skin underneath the soft jogging top, and she pressed against his hard body. As their tongues sought and probed, the flames of passion burst anew within them.

"Does this place have a rug?" he murmured against her lips.

"Um-hmm." Her jogging shirt made a bright green splash on the floor. "Over there." Her jogging pants landed with a muffled whoosh on the back of a straight-backed chair.

"Maggie. It's been years." Adam's belt buckle clattered on the tiled floor.

The sun smiled through the window at them as Adam's lips roamed over Maggie's body, renewing an old acquaintance and making new discoveries. The mist-covered mountains presided in solemn dignity as their bodies at last joined in heart-thundering reunion. The shadows were long on the wall when their mingled cries of satisfaction filled the room. And, outside their window, a mockingbird offered his benediction.

"Adam Trent, I think I'm addicted to you." Maggie smiled down at her beloved, and her hair flowed across his chest in a bright sheaf of gold.

"Maggie Merriweather, I plan to keep it that way." He sat up on the fireside rug and stretched. Suddenly he grimaced and reached underneath him. "What's this?" He was holding her poster.

"Turn it over."

The poster board rattled as Adam turned it over and read the bold black letters—I SURRENDER. His eyebrows shot upward. "Maggie?"

"I was planning to take your bank by storm. Just march right in with my sign and announce to everybody in Tupelo that I love you and that I'm giving up causes."

"I'm sure you were planning to stand on the check-writing table." He grinned at her.

"Of course."

"And it never crossed your mind to come and

knock discreetly on my door?" In the evening shadows of the room, his blue eyes sparkled like sunshine on the Mediterranean.

"Never." She gave him an arch look, and then asked seriously, "Are you sorry?"

"No, Maggie." He hugged her fiercely to him. "I did my damnedest to tame you, and I made two remarkable discoveries."

She reached up and trailed her fingers along his jawline. "And what were they?"

"You can't be tamed." He chuckled and planted a kiss atop her shining hair. "And I wouldn't have it any other way."

She leaned against his shoulder, and together they sat contentedly in front of the fire. The sun disappeared behind a shadowy purple mountain, and the only light in the room was the flickering blaze of the fire in the stone hearth.

"Adam?"

"Hmm?"

"Don't change. I love you just the way you are." She twisted in his arms and looked earnestly up into his face. "You once said that love allows differences."

"I know that, Maggie, but is it a difference you can live with?"

"As long as I have you."

"Maggie, when I wasn't raging like a wounded lion and storming Doc Merriweather's house, I did some serious thinking about us."

"And?"

"I'm not sure I can afford enough silver trumpets for all our kids if their mother persists in her style of protest." His right hand caressed the length of her leg as he talked. "How about channeling all your energy in a different direction and taking on a partner?"

"Who?"

"Me."

"You must be joking!"

"No, I'm not. I know you will always want to fight for the animals, no matter what you think now, and the most effective way to do that is to lobby for legislative changes that need to be made in that area. I'll help you."

"We'll take our horns and storm the governor's office!" Her green eyes sparkled with excitement.

"Without our horns, Tigress." His hand moved up to brush across her swollen nipples.

Maggie sucked in her breath as the heat started in her loins and spread slowly throughout her body. "Agreed. And I have a proposal for you." Her nipples jutted like rosebuds into the palm of his hand as she continued breathlessly. "I want you to donate all the game you bag to the Children's Home, for food." Her voice was becoming thick and husky as his hands worked their magic.

"That sounds like a workable compromise to me. Agreed." He lowered his head and began to plant slow, sensuous kisses across her shoulders and at the nape of her neck. "There's one more thing, Maggie."

Her breath was coming in ragged bursts as she turned to him. "What?"

"On momentous occasions such as this one, the compromise must have a stamp of approval by both parties."

"Like this?" Her breath fanned his cheeks as she lifted soft, yielding lips to his.

"No." He growled. "Like this." And he rolled over her on the rug as they sealed their pact.

They were married on the first day of January in the small brick church in Belden, with all their family as witnesses.

Jim winked broadly as she walked down the aisle on her father's arm. Paul and Martha Trent beamed at their son, and Elijah Jane, who always cried at weddings, sniffled loudly into her handkerchief.

Thirteen gray heads nodded their approval from two pews near the front of the church as the Deerfield Nursing Home residents beamed at Maggie.

Adam stood at the altar waiting for her, his smile lighting her whole world and his eyes promising a lifetime of magic.

As she placed her hand in Adam's in a gesture that would join them forever, she heard Grandmother Trent's pleased stage whisper. "I'll have me a granddaughter now. I know that look in Adam's eyes."

Epilogue

"Go downstairs and light the fire, Elijah Jane." Maggie stood in a patch of sunlight at her bedroom window, her eyes eagerly scanning the curving driveway below for the first sign of Adam's car.

"Light the fiah? On the fo'th of July!" Elijah Jane shook her head. "The saints preserve us." She painstakingly rubbed lemon oil into the bedpost. "What are you up to now?"

Maggie laughed as she watched Beau, Adam's calico cat, chase fat Muffin around a rosebush. It had taken Beauregard only a few days to establish his position as reigning king of the hill after she and her dogs had moved to Adam's house. They kept her cottage as a getaway place. Still laughing, she turned to face Elijah Jane.

Her smile broadened. Elijah Jane had her lips pursed, muttering to herself, but her eyes were glowing with possessive pride. A bright red nightcap sat slightly askew on her grizzled hair—to protect her hair from dust, she said—and her purple blouse was tucked into a shocking-pink skirt. She loved bright colors.

Elijah Jane had been coming every Wednesday since she and Adam had been married, because Grandmother Trent had asked how Maggie could produce a great-granddaughter if she had to bother with less important things, like housework.

"What makes you think I'm up to something?" Maggie's eyes swung back to the driveway, checking.

"You're always up to som'thin'. Decoratin' that Eastah ham with taffy and then you and Mistah Adam disappearin' while we try to find the ham undah that sticky mess! Lordy, Lordy." She tried to keep a stern face, but her lips kept turning up at the corners as she recalled that first big family dinner, when Maggie had cooked and invited all the kin.

"I thought it would be different." In the distance Maggie saw a glimpse of silver as Adam's Mercedes entered the lane of oaks that led to their house.

"Diff'runt's the word for it." Elijah Jane turned to the bedside table and picked up a covered porcelain temple jar. Its contents rattled in her hand. "And keepin' buttons in a jah! Who keeps buttons in a jah?" She opened the top and peered inside. "They look mighty like Mistah Adam's shirt buttons." Her eyes twinkled as she looked at Maggie, then back at the buttons.

Maggie hitched up her army pants as she saw Adam nose his car into the garage. "Hurry, Elijah Jane. Here he comes."

Elijah Jane's hips rolled with every step as she left the room. "Lightin' fiahs on the fo'th of July. Wearin' those baggy britches. Umm-umm." Alternately muttering and chuckling, she flopped down the stairs.

Holding her hand over her hammering heart, Maggie waited upstairs, listening for the first sound of Adam's voice. "Where's my wife, Elijah Jane?"

Maggie held her breath as she listened to his shoes tap against the hardwood floor. Reaching into the closet, she took out a large poster-board sign mounted on a broom handle. Holding the sign aloft, she grabbed her silver trumpet and descended the back stairs.

"Upstaihs," Elijah Jane told Adam as she busied herself at the hearth.

Walking softly, Maggie entered the family room unnoticed and positioned herself behind Adam. Lifting the silver trumpet to her lips, she began playing the opening bars of the *William Tell* overture.

Adam's back stiffened, and he whirled around to stare at her. Elijah Jane continued to light the fire as if nothing had happened.

Adam's eyes rapidly took in the army pants—Maggie's crusading uniform—the silver trumpet, and the sign. "Maggie?" His eyebrows rose in question.

"I've got a new cause, Adam."

"So I see." He stood quietly as he assessed the situation. "Out with it, Tigress. What can we expect this time?"

Maggie whipped the sign around so that Adam could see the printed letters. Her face was wreathed in smiles.

Shock, disbelief, and delight chased across Adam's face. "Is it true, Maggie?"

"Glory be!" yelled Elijah Jane. "We're gonna have a baby!"

Adam closed the small space between himself and Maggie and scooped her into his arms. The "Congratulations, Daddy" sign slipped to the floor as she wound her arms around his neck.

"It's true, Adam."

Adam lifted Maggie off her feet and started

toward the fire. "Elijah Jane, run to the store and get some fresh mushrooms."

"The refrigerator is full of fresh mushrooms. I spied 'em myself."

"Elijah Jane!" Adam roared. "The Blazer keys are on the key board in the kitchen."

"Ev'ry Wednesday it's 'Go get fresh mushrooms.' That man has enough mushrooms in his kitchen to open his own grocery sto'." Elijah Jane was smiling from ear to ear by the time she reached the kitchen door. Behind her came the sound of buttons rolling on the hardwood floor. She banged the door loudly to announce her departure.

In the family room nobody noticed. Adam settled Maggie gently onto the fireside rug. Shivers skittered across her skin as his hands traced her body. "All we need now is a snowstorm," he murmured. His eyes were liquid blue fire as he brought his lips to hers.

"I think I can arrange a storm. Without the snow." Then there was no more time for words. Maggie closed her eyes as the fire that was Adam Trent reached out and consumed her.

Unnoticed, the silver trumpet clanked to the floor and lay among the buttons, glinting in the flames from the Fourth of July fire.

THE EDITOR'S CORNER

Sandra Brown, Iris Johansen and all of us at Bantam Books are delighted by your response to **SUNSET EMBRACE** and **THE FOREVER DREAM**. We thank you most sincerely for not only buying the novels, but for letting us know through your cards and letters how much you liked them. Now, you may want to urge any of your friends who haven't yet got their copies of **SUNSET EMBRACE** to rush to their nearest bookseller to do so. Why? Because they will want to be ready for Sandra's stunning sequel to it, **ANOTHER DAWN,** which we are publishing in October (on sale early in September). Next month we'll run an excerpt in the back of the LOVESWEPTs of this wonderful historical novel that tells the love story of Jake ("Bubba") Langston. **ANOTHER DAWN** is a breathtakingly exciting romance novel that we are very proud to publish.

And speaking of being "proud to publish," that's exactly how we feel about next month's LOVESWEPTs.

That talented author Fayrene Preston is back with the sensual and evocative **RACHEL'S CONFESSION**, LOVESWEPT #107. Rachel Kirkland is a forthright and very lovely young woman. Wounded by a first love, she has vowed to marry for money and she candidly says so to Alex Doral. Very much a man . . . very much a wealthy man, Alex has just arrived in the town to which Rachel also has returned to live with and help take care of her grandmother and her younger sister. Soon, Alex is determined to marry Rachel for he yearns to possess her and to heal the hurts he suspects she carries in her heart. **RACHEL'S CON-**

(continued)

FESSION is one of Fayrene's most compelling romances and you won't want to miss it!

If you thought Billie Green's last LOVESWEPT was wonderful, can you imagine what she'll come up with after **A TOUGH ACT TO FOLLOW,** LOVESWEPT #108? Indeed it's going to be difficult for her to top this witty and touching love story between Dempsey Turner-Riley and James Halloran. Delightfully off-the-wall, Dempsey literally captivates James on first meeting. (I can't leave it at "captivates"; I must tell you that this couple is handcuffed to one another . . . and the key is lost.) And then this fascinating pair is drawn into a madcap caper that sends them on a wild goose chase . . . with the most enchanting prize at the end. **A TOUGH ACT TO FOLLOW** sure is!

We're very, very pleased to introduce you to a marvelous new writer, Laurien Berenson, whose heartwarming romance **COME AS YOU ARE** is LOVESWEPT #109. Gem McAllister is a sensitive, loving young woman whose occupation is the despair of her family. Playing the role of Emerald the Clown, she entertains at parties and on the streets of San Francisco. She could scarcely believe the name of the "boy" she was to awaken with balloons and songs on his birthday. Tom Tucker's name proved to be no joke . . . but "boy" certainly did for he was tall, handsome . . . and, indeed, adult. Together they began to celebrate more than his birthday, yet his rather stuffy background and profession seemed to loom between them. **COME AS YOU ARE** is a tender and touching love story from the zany first to the memorable last.

Last, but certainly not least, we have a beautiful romance from Joan Elliott Pickart, **SUNLIGHT'S PROMISE,** LOVESWEPT #110. Jill Tinsley is poor as a church mouse and proud as a peacock about her independence. When she meets Chip Chandler her life takes an abrupt turn. Chip wants to cherish Jill, to fill her life with all the things she's never had. But Jill finds it impossible to accept anything but love from the man she's fallen for. When her secret dreams begin to come true in her professional life, too, an emotional storm blows up! Watch the secondary characters in this book. One of them has his . . . er, or her own story in Joan's next LOVESWEPT, **RAINBOW'S ANGEL**.

Enjoy!

With every good wish,
Sincerely,

Carolyn Nichols

Carolyn Nichols
   Editor
LOVESWEPT
Bantam Books, Inc.
666 Fifth Avenue
New York, NY 10103

*A special excerpt of
the riveting historical novel
GAMBLER IN LOVE
by bestselling author
PATRICIA MATTHEWS*

THE morning was glorious, clear and sunny, heralding the approach of full summer. It was a day to match Cat's feelings. She woke late, and was for a moment puzzled as to why she felt so good. Then the memory of last night flooded back to her, and she stretched like a contented kitten.

She dressed quickly and went up on deck. Everything seemed sharper this morning—the air smelled like wine; the songs of the birds along the canal bank sounded sweeter than she remembered; and everything she touched had a different feel to it. It was as though her passage into womanhood had sharpened all her senses, and it was wonderful to be alive.

Mick, looking disheveled and hung over, was sitting by the tiller, sipping at a mug of hot tea. Timmie was exercising the mules along the towpath, but Morgan was nowhere to be seen.

"Good morning, Mick. Where's Morgan?"

"How should I know? I'm not the lad's keeper," he said grumpily.

"But haven't you seen him?"

"Nope. He didn't even sleep in the cabin last night. Leastways, he wasn't in his bunk when I came back, about midnight. Never did show up." He gave her a look edged with malice. "Maybe the boyo decided he'd had enough of canal life, and snuck away in the night."

Hiding her alarm as best she could, Cat said, "Did he take his things?"

"What things? All the bucko has is the clothes he was wearing." He gestured and turned away, without looking at her again. "I'm thinking it's good riddance if he is gone."

She opened her mouth to retort hotly, but she refrained, afraid that she might give herself away if she said too much.

She turned away and mounted the towpath, staring up toward the town. Her good spirits had vanished. Cat knew that if Morgan *had* left, she would miss him sorely. But would he just sneak away in the night? That was not like him. . . .

And then she saw him striding along the towpath toward her. Her heart gave a great leap of joy, but she had herself composed by the time he reached her.

"Good morning, my dear," he said gravely, his eyes searching hers. "How are you this grand morning?"

"I'm fine," she said in a neutral voice. "I was just wondering where you were."

"I had things to do. I've been searching for a cargo for the *Cat*."

"Did you find anything?"

He nodded, smiling. "Oh, yes, a load of grain. I took it at a price lower than the going rate. I hope you don't mind. I figured that was better than going back empty."

Gambler in Love

"I don't mind at all; I think it's wonderful. You're a born canawler, Morgan!" She experienced a sudden desire to reach out and touch him, and then he spoiled it.

"The wagons will be here in about"—he took out his watch—"an hour."

"You were pretty sure of yourself, weren't you?" she said testily. "I gave you no authority to make such decisions!"

"But you just agreed that it was a good deal," he pointed out.

"All right, all right. But next time you might consult me first."

"I had to act quickly, Cat. Two other canal-boat owners came in while I was there. If I'd left to consult with you, without an agreement being reached, the grain merchant might have given the cargo to one of the others."

Knowing that he was right did not wholly appease her, but she said nothing more; instead, she turned toward the boat, calling out, "Timmie, get the mules fed. We have a cargo coming, and will be departing before too long."

Soon wagons began pulling in alongside the boat. They all pitched in, and five wagonloads of grain were soon stored below. Cat was introduced to the grain merchant, a plump, harried-looking individual named Fredricks.

"This man of yours, Miss Carnahan," Fredricks said, "is a pretty convincing fellow. If he hadn't been, I might have given my grain to another hauler. One man there offered to haul it much cheaper, but I'd already agreed to let you have it. I hope I don't have cause to regret my decision."

Cat felt her face flush at the phrase *this man of yours*, but she returned the merchant's gaze steadily and said, "You won't have cause to regret it, Mr. Fredricks, I promise you."

As they got under way, Morgan came to Cat at the tiller and said, "You know who one of those other two canawlers was? I'm sure he was the one who offered the lower rate. It was Simon Maphis."

"Maphis? And you beat him at his own game? Oh, I could kiss you for that, Morgan!"

"Why not?" he said jauntily, glancing around. "No one's looking."

Cat turned to tilt her face up to his, and he kissed her full on the mouth.

Cat selected a small side-cut, and they tied up there shortly after sundown. She watched Morgan help Timmie stable the mules, while Mick went below to prepare supper. She studied Morgan covertly, watching his well-muscled body in graceful movement, observing the sure quickness of his hands; and she shivered slightly as she remembered those hands on her body last night.

For the first time in a long while, she felt relaxed, without concern about where their next cargo was coming from. She felt confident that Morgan would always manage to find them something to earn money. Although she had little faith in luck—in her opinion, a person made his own luck—she had the feeling that the presence of Morgan Kane on board the boat was a talisman of a brighter future.

Her thoughts were interrupted as she saw Morgan coming along the towpath toward where she sat by the tiller. He made the jump onto the boat easily; and watching him, Cat suddenly wanted him, a want that was a sweet ache. She wanted to be in his arms again; she wanted again what she had experienced last night. He stopped before her, and as she looked up, his face went still, his eyes staring down into hers; and she realized that her want

Gambler in Love

must be naked on her face. At that moment she did not care; she wanted him to know!

"Cat ..." He reached out to touch her, and then the moment was shattered by the sound of a bell clanging on the canal. With a start Morgan glanced around at a small boat hurrying east, pulled by a team of four horses. A bell hung on the bow, and a man was standing beside it. Even as Morgan watched, he clanged it again.

"What the hell is *that*?"

Cat laughed. "That is a hurry-up boat."

"And what is a hurry-up boat?"

"Troubleshooting boats. There's either a breach upstream in the berm or the towpath. Or they could be going to the rescue of a 'mudlark.' And before you ask, a mudlark is any boat that has run aground."

Morgan's attention returned to her again, but before he could speak, Mick's head poked up from below. "Food's ready, folks! Shall we eat on deck, as usual?"

Struggling for composure, Cat nodded. "Of course, Mick." She started to rise. "I'll help you bring it up."

"No, you sit there." Morgan's hand closed on her shoulder, squeezing intimately, his burning gaze still locked with hers. "I'll help your father."

The wine and the simple but hearty food that Mick had prepared further relaxed Cat. She sat quietly, listening with amusement as her father told Morgan tall tales about the Erie, a sure indication that Mick not only accepted Morgan as one of them but that he liked the man.

"There was this mad sea captain," Mick said, "who spent good money for a dead whale that had been washed up on a Cape Cod beach. Now this bucko figured that he was going to get rich off'n that dead creature, by showing it to people along the Erie, charging a goodly fee, o'course. Trouble was, after the thing had been out in the sun for a week or so, it began to stink something terrible. Nobody would go within a hundred yards of this feller's boat, much less pay to go and see the bloody carcass. The captain tried to get rid of the stinking carcass by dumping it into the canal at night. But a canal walker spotted him, reported him, and the captain was fined two dollars for interfering with canal traffic. You know what finally happened?" Mick laughed uproariously. "He found a farmer about as mad as he was, and convinced him that the whale would make good fertilizer for his crops. He sold the whale to him for eight cents! Jaysus, no telling how much that captain was out of pocket, towing that great carcass all that way!"

Morgan laughed appreciatively, and Cat joined in, although she had heard the story many times. Morgan's glance met hers, and again Cat felt the stirring of desire. She moved restlessly, hoping that Morgan would make some move to get her alone.

When Mick had finally run out of steam, and had taken the dishes down to the galley, Morgan said, "Would you like to walk for a little, Cat? It's a nice night, and we might sleep better for a bit of a stroll."

Cat rose to her feet eagerly. "I'd like that very much, Morgan."

She took Morgan's arm, and they strolled along the towpath. There was a slice of a moon, which gave a little light filtering through the trees shadowing the path. Insects hummed in the warm darkness, and somewhere a frog croaked hoarsely.

Morgan said, "I do believe that Mick is coming around to approving of me, finally."

Cat smiled up at him. "You can be sure of it. When he banters with someone like he did with you tonight, he likes that someone."

Gambler in Love

"Well, the feeling is mutual, Cat. I like your father."

"I like him, too, most of the time." She sighed plaintively. "If only he'd ease off on the drink."

Morgan shrugged. "Well, we all have our faults, some to a greater degree than others."

"And you, you seem to have taken to canal life well enough. Have you given any more thought to how long you'll stay with us?" She held her breath for his answer.

"I think I'll stick around for a while." He squeezed her arm.

"But what if your memory comes back and you find you're ... Well, if you find you're an important man somewhere, with a good job and responsibilities?"

"Somehow I'm sure I don't have any responsibilities, nothing to take me away from the Erie, and you, if I chose to stay."

"I'm glad you feel that way, Morgan." Her breath was coming fast, and her heartbeat was erratic.

Morgan turned them back toward the boat, and he did not speak again until they neared the side-cut. "Shall we walk over in that direction, toward that glade?"

She nodded mutely, already anticipating what was about to happen. Her body turned soft and hot with need. She wanted this man with an intensity that she would not have thought possible.

"There's one bad thing about canal boats," he said in a low voice. "They're so cramped, there's almost no privacy."

"I know," she said, detesting the tremble in her voice.

He led her into the secluded area and under a spreading tree. Cupping her face between his hands, he kissed her, lightly at first. She came against him hard, returning his kiss with ardor, hands pressing his back.

"Dear, sweet Cat," Morgan murmured. "You have been

Gambler in Love

in my thoughts all day, and I would become passionate just thinking about last night."

"I know. Me, too," she said shakily.

He stepped back from her, and removed his coat, spreading it on the thick grass. Cat sank to her knees on it, and Morgan dropped down beside her, taking her into his arms again. They embraced like that, swaying back and forth in their mounting passion.

She quickly divested herself of her trousers, shirt, and undergarments, then lay with pounding heart while he undressed. His tall, muscular body had the look of a statue, dappled by the moonlight filtering through the leaves. Somehow, being out in the open like this, with the night like a warm pulse beating around them, made it seem more natural to Cat, completely without any coloring of shame.

Then he was beside her, his hands on her body, his mouth on hers.

She locked her arms around his shoulders, and held him imprisoned there, his wildness restricted by her women's strength. As her pleasure increased, Cat became abandoned, her wildness matching his own. Morgan groaned loudly, his arms tightening around her as he began to shudder out his ecstasy.

"Ah, my sweet Cat, my sweet wanton, how I love you!"

When he finally lay beside her, she said musingly, "You called me wanton, Morgan. Am I?"

"I think so, but I meant it in the nicest sense, and there's nothing wrong with that. It's as it should be, and I love you the more for it."

She stirred uneasily. "But, a wanton ... A woman who is that is not considered a good woman. Landsmen think of most canal women as wantons, or tarts."

He traced the line of her jaw with his finger. "Ah, but

Gambler in Love

wanton can mean many other things. It can mean playful, capricious, unrestrained, and you are all those things. Besides, names mean very little. It's a label people put on other people they don't like, or understand. It's what people feel about themselves that truly matters. Do you feel like a *bad* woman?"

She thought for a moment. "No, I feel good about myself, I feel good about what's happened to me." Blushing furiously, she hid her face in the crook of her shoulder.

"Then it's all right, isn't it? Besides, love, you told me, many times, that you care little about what other people think of you."

"But this is something different. I just didn't want you to think that I'm . . ."

"Hush." He covered her mouth with his hand. "I think you're the best woman I've ever known, and I love you."

There was an expectant pause, and Cat knew that he wanted her to answer in kind; but she could not, not just yet. She stirred and sat up. "It grows late, and Mick and Timmie will soon begin to wonder. We'd best get back."

"As you wish, Cat." There was an edge of disappointment in his voice.

He got up, picked up his clothes, and began to dress. In a few minutes they were ready to go back, and Cat took his arm as they strolled back toward the boat, both silent, busy with their own thoughts.

Climbing up the towpath, they soon could see the *Cat*. The boat was dark, and Cat assumed that both Mick and Timmie were bedded down for the night, for which she was glad; she was positive that there was a glow about her, and Mick could surmise from one look at her what had just occurred.

Then she stopped, blinking, and pulled at Morgan's arm. "What's that glow?"

Gambler in Love

Morgan followed the direction of her pointing finger. "Fire, it must be fire!"

He began to run, with Cat right on his heels. As they drew near, Cat saw a dark figure squatting in the shallow water by the bow. Even as she watched, she saw the figure toss a pail of liquid against the boat, and the fire flared. The *Cat* was on fire; someone was putting the torch to her!

By the year 2000, 2 out of 3 Americans could be illiterate.

It's true.

Today, 75 million adults... about one American in three, can't read adequately. And by the year 2000, U.S. News & World Report envisions an America with a literacy rate of only 30%.

Before that America comes to be, you can stop it... by joining the fight against illiteracy today.

Call the Coalition for Literacy at toll-free **1-800-228-8813** and volunteer.

Volunteer Against Illiteracy. The only degree you need is a degree of caring.

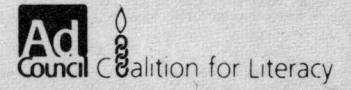

Ad Council Coalition for Literacy

LWA

LOVESWEPT

Love Stories you'll never forget by authors you'll always remember

☐	21637	Love, Catch a Wild Bird #28 Anne Reisser	$1.95
☐	21626	The Lady and the Unicorn #29 Iris Johansen	$1.95
☐	21628	Winner Take All #30 Nancy Holder	$1.95
☐	21635	The Golden Valkyrie #31 Iris Johansen	$1.95
☐	21638	C.J.'s Fate #32 Kay Hooper	$1.95
☐	21639	The Planting Season #33 Dorothy Garlock	$1.95
☐	21629	For Love of Sami #34 Fayrene Preston	$1.95
☐	21627	The Trustworthy Redhead #35 Iris Johansen	$1.95
☐	21636	A Touch of Magic #36 Carla Neggers	$1.95
☐	21641	Irresistible Forces #37 Marie Michael	$1.95
☐	21642	Temporary Angel #38 Billie Green	$1.95
☐	21646	Kirsten's Inheritance #39 Joan Domning	$2.25
☐	21645	Return to Santa Flores #40 Iris Johansen	$2.25
☐	21656	The Sophisticated Mountain Gal #41 Joan Bramsch	$2.25
☐	21655	Heat Wave #42 Sara Orwig	$2.25
☐	21649	To See the Daisies . . . First #43 Billie Green	$2.25
☐	21648	No Red Roses #44 Iris Johansen	$2.25
☐	21644	That Old Feeling #45 Fayrene Preston	$2.25
☐	21650	Something Different #46 Kay Hooper	$2.25

Prices and availability subject to change without notice.

Buy them at your local bookstore or use this handy coupon for ordering:

Bantam Books, Inc., Dept. SW2, 414 East Golf Road, Des Plaines, Ill. 60016

Please send me the books I have checked above. I am enclosing $_____
(please add $1.25 to cover postage and handling). Send check or money order
—no cash or C.O.D.'s please.

Mr/Mrs/Miss_____

Address_____

City_____ State/Zip_____

SW2—6/85

Please allow four to six weeks for delivery. This offer expires 12/85.

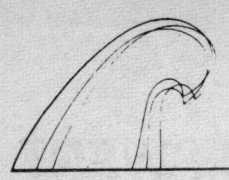

LOVESWEPT

Love Stories you'll never forget by authors you'll always remember

☐	21657	The Greatest Show on Earth #47 Nancy Holder	$2.25
☐	21658	Beware the Wizard #48 Sara Orwig	$2.25
☐	21660	The Man Next Door #49 Kathleen Downes	$2.25
☐	21633	In Search of Joy #50 Noelle Berry McCue	$2.25
☐	21659	Send No Flowers #51 Sandra Brown	$2.25
☐	21652	Casey's Cavalier #52 Olivia & Ken Harper	$2.25
☐	21654	Little Consequences #53 Barbara Boswell	$2.25
☐	21653	The Gypsy & the Yachtsman #54 Joan J. Domning	$2.25
☐	21664	Capture the Rainbow #55 Iris Johansen	$2.25
☐	21662	Encore #56 Kimberly Wagner	$2.25
☐	21640	Unexpected Sunrise #57 Helen Mittermeyer	$2.25
☐	21663	Oregon Brown #58 Sara Orwig	$2.25
☐	21665	Touch the Horizon #59 Iris Johansen	$2.25
☐	21666	When You Speak Love #60 B. J. James	$2.25
☐	21667	Breaking All the Rules #61 Joan Elliott Pickart	$2.25
☐	21668	Pepper's Way #62 Kay Hooper	$2.25
☐	21634	Lahti's Apple #63 Joan J. Domning	$2.25
☐	21670	A Kiss to Make It Better #64 Joan Bramsch	$2.25
☐	21673	The Last Hero #65 Billie Green	$2.25
☐	21672	In a Class By Itself #66 Sandra Brown	$2.25
☐	21669	Vortex #67 Helen Mittermeyer	$2.25
☐	21676	Undercover Affair #68 Helen Conrad	$2.25
☐	21677	The Queen's Defense #69 Marianne Shock	$2.25
☐	21675	The Midnight Special #70 Sara Orwig	$2.25
☐	21678	If There Be Dragons #71 Kay Hooper	$2.25
☐	21687	Probable Cause #72 Sandra Kleinschmit	$2.25
☐	21680	More Than Friends #73 B. J. James	$2.25
☐	21681	Charade #74 Joan Elliott Pickart	$2.25

Prices and availability subject to change without notice.

Buy them at your local bookstore or use this handy coupon for ordering:

Bantam Books, Inc., Dept. SW3, 414 East Golf Road, Des Plaines, Ill. 60016

Please send me the books I have checked above. I am enclosing $_____
(please add $1.25 to cover postage and handling). Send check or money order
—no cash or C.O.D.'s please.

Mr/Mrs/Miss _____

Address _____

City _____ State/Zip _____

SW3—8/85

Please allow four to six weeks for delivery. This offer expires 12/85.

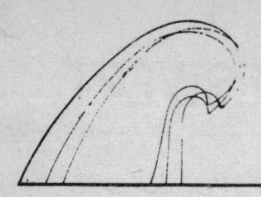

Love Stories you'll never forget by authors you'll always remember

☐	21682	The Count from Wisconsin #75 Billie Green	$2.25
☐	21683	Tailor-Made #76 Elizabeth Barrett	$2.25
☐	21684	Finders Keepers #77 Nancy Holder	$2.25
☐	21688	Sensuous Perception #78 Barbara Boswell	$2.25
☐	21686	Thursday's Child #79 Sandra Brown	$2.25
☐	21691	The Finishing Touch #80 Joan Elliott Pickart	$2.25
☐	21685	The Light Side #81 Joan Bramsch	$2.25
☐	21689	White Satin #82 Iris Johansen	$2.25
☐	21690	Illegal Possession #83 Kay Hooper	$2.25
☐	21693	A Stranger Called Adam #84 B. J. James	$2.25
☐	21700	All the Tomorrows #85 Joan Elliott Pickart	$2.25
☐	21692	Blue Velvet #86 Iris Johansen	$2.25
☐	21661	Dreams of Joe #87 Billie Green	$2.25
☐	21702	At Night Fall #88 Joan Bramsch	$2.25
☐	21694	Captain Wonder #89 Anne Kolaczyk	$2.25
☐	21703	Look for the Sea Gulls #90 Joan Elliott Pickart	$2.25
☐	21704	Calhoun and Kid #91 Sara Orwig	$2.25
☐	21705	Azure Days, Quicksilver Nights #92 Carole Douglas	$2.25
☐	21697	Practice Makes Perfect #93 Kathleen Downes	$2.25
☐	21706	Waiting for Prince Charming #94 Joan Elliott Pickart	$2.25

Prices and availability subject to change without notice.

Buy them at your local bookstore or use this handy coupon for ordering:

Bantam Books, Inc., Dept. SW4, 414 East Golf Road, Des Plaines, Ill. 60016

Please send me the books I have checked above. I am enclosing
$_____ (please add $1.25 to cover postage and handling). Send check or money order—no cash or C.O.D.'s please.

Mr/Ms_____

Address_____

City/State_____ Zip_____

SW4—8/85

Please allow four to six weeks for delivery. This offer expires 2/86.